Antony

TALES FROM TARTARY

Russian Tales · Volume 2

With love from
Uncle Brian.

Christmas 1948.

TALES FROM TARTARY

RUSSIAN TALES · VOLUME TWO

Retold by James Riordan

ILLUSTRATED BY ANTHONY COLBERT

KESTREL BOOKS / LONDON

THE VIKING PRESS / NEW YORK

KESTREL BOOKS
Published by Penguin Books Ltd
Harmondsworth, Middlesex, England

First published 1978
Text Copyright © 1978 by James Riordan
Illustrations Copyright © 1978 by Anthony Colbert

THE VIKING PRESS
First published in the USA in 1979 by The Viking Press
625 Madison Avenue, New York, NY 10022

U.K. ISBN 0 7226 5362 X

Library of Congress Cataloging in Publication Data

Riordan, James, 1936–
    Tales from Tartary.

    (His Russian tales; v. 2)
    SUMMARY: Thirty-nine folktales from the
Tartar region of Russia.
    1. Tales, Russian. [1. Folklore – Russia]
    I. Turska, Krystyna, 1933–   II. – Title.
PZ81.R4495Ru vol. 2 [398.2]   77–27871
U.S. ISBN 0–670–69156–9

Printed in Great Britain by
Butler & Tanner Ltd, Frome and London

To Rashida
and our children, Salavat, Onara and Gulnara,
that they might know the legends
of their ancestors

Contents

[7]

Contents

I had a vision as I drowsed,
A dream that pleasure gave:
A tale I had recounted roused
My father from his grave.

He heard my song with eyes aglow
Then sang me one of his,
And lo! Chingis's ghost arose
Beside the deep abyss.

Chingis appeared and sang a song
That long ago was born,
And Tartar kinsmen there did throng
To listen till the dawn.

Young Tartar who shall follow me
When in damp earth I'm pressed,
Awake me with your poetry
That I might lie at rest.

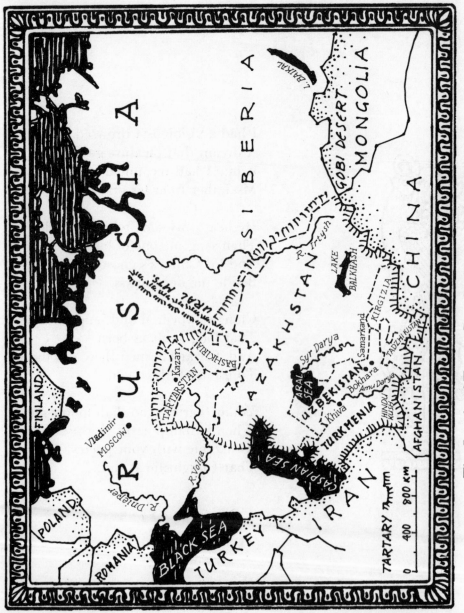

The Lands of Tartar Peoples in the USSR Today

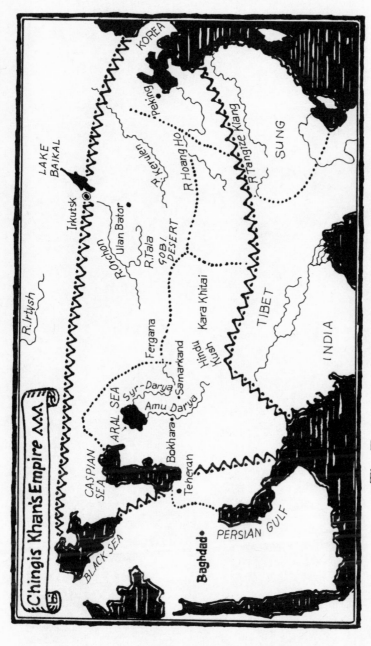

The Tartar Empire in the Thirteenth Century

Yerensay's Forty Fables

A GREAT and haughty Tartar khan was very fond of stories. He would listen for hours to tales of adventure, long verses of the heroes of his clan, religious sermons about Mohamed the Prophet and favourite of all were the clever fables that rang as true as life.

But, like the desert streams in summer, in the course of time the story-tellers at court ran dry. And the khan became so miserable he issued a proclamation:

> I, Chingis Khan, by the grace of Allah,
> do declare
> that I shall grant half my Khanate, and
> my Daughter, to the Man who can tell me
> *FORTY FABLES*

As you may divine, dear listener, many young men took up the challenge. First came the merchants:

'After all, we trick our clients a hundred times a day!' they reasoned. 'It will surely not be hard to tell a mere forty fables...'

So one after the other they came before the khan to claim their reward, half the khanate (you see, dear listener, gold was what they sought, not the khan's lovely daughter).

Alas, the yarns they spun were so boring that none could tell even as many as twenty original stories. So, with a yawn and a sigh, the great khan had their heads removed. All and every one.

Next came the mullahs from the mosques. They were used to weaving all manner of fanciful tales to the faithful; so surely they could tell a trifling forty fables. Alas. Once they had exhausted the sacred tales from

[13]

the life of the Prophet, they were at a loss – for they had never learnt any other stories.

Thus the khan's executioner tied each unfortunate mullah securely in a sack and threw them all into a lake.

(You see, dear listener, the khan – being a pious man – deemed it sinful to cut off the mullahs' heads.)

Presently a young man – neither merchant nor mullah – presented himself to the khan.

'My name is Yerensay,' he announced. 'I can tell the great and mighty khan forty stories from my own life.'

'What do you mean, you miserable dog, from your own life?' exclaimed the khan. 'Don't waste my time. I want only fables!'

'The great khan is merciful and compassionate,' answered the young man with a bow. 'I have heard folk say our lives are nought but a dream ... Who would say what is true and what a fable?'

'Aha!' exclaimed the khan. 'Here's a man who bears the mark of a true storyteller. Talk on, unworthy one. And, if you manage even half the fables, I shall be merciful – instead of your head I shall remove just your eyes!'

'The khan's kindness knows no bounds,' replied Yerensay. 'But I wish to be assured that my stories will be counted. Is there an honest man in the khan's household who can count to forty?'

'Waste no more words, son of a camel!' exploded the khan in a fury. 'My vizier will count your lies and I myself will make doubly certain.'

'The great khan is wise and all-seeing,' said Yerensay, 'but, when the vizier keeps count, doubtless no more than half reaches the khan's ears.'

'Executioner!' screamed the khan, losing patience. 'Prepare the rope to hang this lump of camel-dung!'

'Wait, O fount of wisdom, stay your rope,' said Yerensay hastily, 'I am now beginning my tale.'

'Then make haste,' shouted the khan, 'for I have a mind to hang you before dusk.'

[14]

'Ah, Son of the Sun,' began the storyteller, 'I must start my adventures in days gone by, a long, long time ago . . .'

'Never mind, never mind!' broke in the khan. 'You may begin even on that miserable day when you were born. But get on with it.'

'Oh no, wise khan! That I cannot do. For a whole half year before my birth a rich bai hired me to tend his horses.'

'One!' counted the vizier. 'That will certainly count as a fable.'

'Yes, he commences boldly,' agreed the khan. 'Let us listen further.'

'Now, in that herd', continued Yerensay, 'all the horses were fleet of foot and they elected the fastest among them to be their leader. A hornless cow no less. The bai was very fond of this cow, which had borne him several colts. But, one day, the hornless cow wandered from the herd – without my noticing it.'

'Two!' said the vizier. 'I have never seen a cow in a herd of horses – let alone its leader!'

'Well, he did say the cow had no horns,' grumbled the khan. 'We know not whether this idiot knows a cow from a horse!'

'The great khan sees deep into men's minds, his wisdom lifts the gloom from our hearts,' said Yerensay. 'May I continue?'

'Yes, yes, go on!' snapped the khan.

'Well, so there it was: the cow had strayed and I rushed across the plain to look for her. So quickly did I run that I stumbled and fell on the top of a mountain . . .'

'Three and a half!' said the vizier.

'Give him his four!' shouted the khan. 'Lest he say we stole a half from him.'

'Let it be three,' broke in Yerensay. 'I'm not greedy. I shall gladly start again should the great khan desire . . .'

'Get on with it,' roared the khan.

'You see,' continued Yerensay, 'in my haste I forgot to put on my boots; I was carrying them in my hands. That's how I came to stub my toe on the mountaintop. And, when I picked myself up and looked down the mountain, I could just see the hoof of the hornless

[15]

cow (the grass at the foot of the mountain hid the rest of her from view).

'Without more ado, I unhitched my lasso, stood it on end and climbed to the very top of it – to have a good view of the cow. But it was no use. What was I to do? Then I recalled that my mother had left a needle behind my ear when she had sewn me a jacket. So I pulled it out, stuck it into my heel, stood on it and could see the cow quite plainly. She was wallowing in a patch of burdock.

'Now you won't get far, my beauty! I said to myself, jumping down from the lasso. But I was unmindful of the needle in my heel! As I landed, the needle went straight through my body and – would you believe it! – came out behind my ear again!

'Just at that moment, a hare darted out from under my feet. He was so plump that fat was oozing from his shiny skin. Snatching up a stick, I threw it at him ...'

'And missed?' asked the khan.

'No, why should I miss?' asked Yerensay. 'Only the stick was too short, and the hare raced on as if nothing had happened. In a rage, I spat after him and killed him outright with my spit!'

'That hare had probably heard your stories,' said the khan, 'and died laughing!'

'More likely as not,' replied Yerensay. 'There is none to compare with the great khan in wit and humour. Perhaps that hare did take a liking to my jokes and indeed died laughing. What a pity I cannot make the vizier laugh!'

'Leave my vizier in peace and continue your story,' ordered the khan. 'Little time enough remains till sundown.'

'So there I was,' said Yerensay, taking up the tale. 'Having killed the hare, I now set off after the hornless cow; but a broad stream blocked my path and I had no way of crossing it. What was I to do? From my knife-handle, I cut a boat and sailed across in that; since I had no oars, I had to whip the stern with my belt to make the boat move faster. Even so, by the time I reached the bank, it was already dusk and I decided to make camp for the night. Before sleeping, I greased my boots with the hare's fat...'

'You didn't say you took the hare with you,' interjected the khan.

'I crave pardon, O great and mighty khan. You see, I took two and a half potfuls of lard from the hare's carcass; there was hardly room for it all in my story, especially as the pots had neither tops nor bottoms.'

'But what did you do with the hare's hide?' asked the khan.

'I cast it away, O munificent khan. You see, as I was skinning that hare, it crawled out of its hide and the skin came apart at the seams.'

'Eeehh Allah!' sighed the khan. 'I'll ask no more questions – otherwise we'll never get to the end of the story!'

'As the great khan pleases,' said Yerensay. 'But, before I finish my tale of the hornless cow, I must relate the story of my boots.

'Well, I only managed to grease one before I fell asleep – so weary was I from the chase. And in the morning I was awakened by a terrible rumpus... I jumped up, rubbing my eyes – and saw my boots fighting! The ungreased one – the left boot – had leaped upon the one with the fat. No sooner did the jealous boot see me awake than he took fright and scampered off. Keeping my wits, I thrust both feet into the remaining boot, caught up with the bully and punished him by putting him on my right foot!'

'Hmmm!' grunted the khan.

'Hmmm!' echoed the vizier.

'Does the great khan wish to say something?' asked Yerensay.

'No, no, nothing! Get on with it,' said the khan.

'Then, perhaps the vizier wishes to speak?'

'I would say one thing,' began the vizier. 'You've already earned the noose around your wretched neck. Twenty fables in one!'

'I knew it!' shouted Yerensay. 'The vizier has already missed a good dozen!'

'Don't lie,' burst in the khan. 'I myself have been keeping count. The score is correct!'

'So be it,' said Yerensay. 'When the great khan speaks, all hear and

obey. But, if it please Your Majesty, I would beg a last chance to save myself from my deserved death.'

'Continue, cow offal!'

'I now wish to tell you what happened on the second day of my chase after the hornless cow. From all that running, I became thirsty – you see, all day long the sun had roasted me like a dry fig. As I ran along, I saw a lake and made for it. Yet, as I bent down to drink, I found the water frozen! I set to hacking the ice with my whip handle. It was no use.

'Then I banged it with my lasso, but only a tiny crack appeared in the ice. At that, I really lost my temper: I tore the head off my shoulders and smashed it onto the ice with such force that ice-chips flew to all sides!

'I drank my fill until the lake grew quite shallow. Mindful of the run-away cow, I leaped up and continued the chase; yet as I pursued the cow I felt the back of my head smouldering in the sun and, when I pushed my hat back, it fell over my shoulders!

'Then I realized: my head was missing!

'I had left it behind by the lake. Being too weary to return for it, I resorted to cunning: I built a fire and pretended to be cooking bish-barmak, describing all the delicious odours and sights: "What a fine dish ... how delicious it smells!"

'My stomach, empty since the previous day, could bear this no longer and began to rumble and squeal with hunger. Thereupon I again spoke up: "Eee-eee! The guests will eat up all my bish-barmak and there will be none left for me. I cannot eat a scrap without my mouth that is in my head that I left by the lake..."

'My stomach was so scared at missing the meal that... whoosh! it jumped out of my body and raced off to fetch my head from the lakeside. By and by, it came back, dragging the head along by the ears. Then, putting my stomach in place and my head back on my shoulders, I put on my hat and set off once more. Oy-yoi-yoi! How that stomach cursed me for tricking it like that!

'At that very instant I noticed an eagle in the sky carrying something in its talons – my hornless cow! What a calamity! What was I to do? The bai would never forgive me for losing his favourite cow. I could not return without the cow – yet now I could not return with the cow!

'I pondered long and hard: how could I outwit the bai? At last I had the answer.

'Very simple.

[19]

'I would not be born! And, from that day to this, I go about unborn.'

After a long pause, the vizier whispered something in the khan's ear, and turned to Yerensay.

'Very well. That's splendid!' said the vizier. 'For a moment I thought we really would have to give you half the khanate for those stupid stories.'

'What are you talking about, fox's droppings?' cried Yerensay. 'Have I not told the khan full forty fables – and another dozen into the bargain (which you, vizier, tried to cheat me of!)? Where is my reward?'

'Reward?' said the khan with a roar of laughter. 'You will receive your reward, my friend...when you are born! For the present, peace be with you. It is time for my evening prayers...'

With that the khan left the chamber, well satisfied with himself and his resourceful vizier.

Shuralee the Wood Demon

THERE is an aul close by Kazan in Tartary – Kurlai by name. Even the hens there trill like nightingales. But in the pine-woods about that aul dwell jinns and evil shuralees who hold their counsels in its shady groves.

But is that really true, you ask? Dear reader, I will swear to you: the great dark forest of Tartary is as boundless as the heavens and, like the heavens, it holds as many purple mysteries within its soul.

It is of one such mystery I wish to tell you. It began late one evening, when the moon was gliding serenely through the sky, casting a pale light upon the forest track. A woodman was on his way to the forest for fire-wood. Arriving at a clearing, he marked out a stout spruce and began to swing his axe:

Tuk-a-tuk-tuk.

Tuk-a-tuk-tuk.

The chips flew as he bit deeper and deeper into the trunk.

As it often is in summer, the night was fresh and moist; and, with the birds and beasts in slumber, all was silent save the rhythmic ringing of the axe. Our woodman was busy about his task when, all of a sudden,

'Chooo-ooo-ooooo!'

A shrill, mocking scream rang out, quite near by.

The woodman froze in terror.

Looking furtively round, his gaze met a most unearthly sight: was that figure human? Was it a jinn or rogue or ghost, that bony beast? What a hideous sight!

It had a fish-hook for a nose; arms and legs like hoary twigs, knotted and gnarled. Its eyes glinted evilly, protruding from its gaunt, greenish face.

[21]

It had a human form – yet it was not human. It was very skinny with a bony head and a horn jutting out about the size of a man's thumb. Its arms hung down half a yard, with ten spindly fingers, sharp and long.

The woodman screwed up his courage and looked straight into those hideous eyes that burned like two crimson fires.

'What do you want of me?' he asked.

'Fear me not,' it replied. 'I shall not tear thee limb from limb. Yet, though I am no brigand, neither am I holy saint. Why, dost thou ask, did I give out a merry scream on seeing thee? Because, dear boy, I tickle folk to death ... Each of my fingers is made to scratch and tickle most wickedly. Come, dear boy, and play a game of tickle with me.'

Seeing he had no choice, the woodman pretended to agree.

'All right, I'll play. But you, wood demon or forest goat – whatever you are – must first help me fell this hefty tree in the middle of the clearing. Take hold where I have cut a wedge; push when I shout.'

Screeching and tittering, the shuralee took up its position: it put its spindly fingers into the cut in the tree to take a firm grip – as the woodman had said. (O wise reader, have you divined the woodman's plan?)

Taking up the wedge that his axe had cut from the tree, the woodman – quick as a toad's tongue – drove it back into the tree, jamming the creature's fingers fast.

Shuralee saw the trick – too late. It hollered and shrieked and called to its brothers for aid, summoning up all the spirits of the forest. But none came.

In cringing tones, it begged the human:

'Take pity, take pity on me, dear boy; pray, let me go. Neither thee, nor thy son, nor thy son's son will I touch. O human, never shall I harm any of thy brethren. I give thee my word.'

Shuralee pushed and pulled, whined and wailed for all it was worth. But the woodman took no notice and got ready to leave. The creature begged him even more.

'Who art thou, heartless one? On the morrow, should I live to meet a fellow creature, who shall I say played me such a cruel trick?'

'I shall tell you my name,' answered the woodman. 'And mark it well. They call me Thistimelastyear ... Now I must be off.'

Shuralee wailed and gnashed its horrible teeth, mustering all its strength to escape and punish the woodman. Yet it could not.

'Forest demons, come to my aid! I was wedged in by Thistimelastyear. He left me to die, Thistimelastyear!'

Only next morning did shuralees come running into the clearing, shouting at their foolish brother:

'Why do you roar and rant so? Your cries jar our ears. If you got stuck this time last year, why do you complain about it only now?'

Aldar-Kose and Shigai-Bai

In times gone by there dwelt in the steppe-lands a poor young man, Aldar-Kose. Save his old grey horse, he had no possessions to his name; all the same, he was a clever storyteller and always had a good store of tricks to play on people.

Now in the same steppe-lands lived a well-to-do man by the name of Shigai-Bai – a thoroughly miserly fellow. Such was his meanness that he would refuse a guest even the thinnest slice of bread or the tiniest drop of goat's milk.

So the cunning Aldar-Kose decided to pay the miser and his family a visit. His neighbours mocked him when they heard:

'Just you wait and see, Aldar-Kose,' they laughed, 'Shigai-Bai will welcome you with open arms; he'll treat you to a feast of mutton-fat and mare's milk. Mind you don't gorge yourself sick! Ha-ha-ha!'

'We shall see,' was the poor man's reply as he rode out across the plains.

Wherever he rode looking for Shigai-Bai's yurta, he found that the miser had already moved on – so scared was he of having unwanted guests! For many days Aldar-Kose journeyed on until at last he sighted a solitary yurta surrounded by thick rushes.

'That must be Shigai-Bai's home,' he thought. 'Only he would place his yurta so that the rustling of the rushes would warn him of visitors; thus he can quickly hide his food.'

And indeed he was right.

Aldar-Kose set to thinking: how could he pass unnoticed through the rushes? At last he hit on a plan. Tying up his old grey horse, he began to gather pebbles until finally he had a large pile. As soon as it grew dark, he began to toss the pebbles one by one into the thick of the rushes. At the sound of the swishing, Shigai-Bai dashed out and looked around.

'Who's there?' he called.

All was quiet. So Shigai-Bai, thinking it must be the wind, went back into his yurta.

No sooner had he disappeared from view than Aldar-Kose threw another stone into the rushes. And again Shigai-Bai rushed out, looked to all sides and strained his ears.

'It is only the wind whistling through the rushes,' he decided. And no more did he run out into the night.

That was exactly what Aldar-Kose wanted. He now took his horse by the reins and led it stealthily through the rushes. He would take a step, stop and listen, take another, then halt and wait again.

In this way he succeeded in reaching the miser's tent without even rousing him. Lifting the thick felt, he peered in. What splendour met his gaze. Thick Persian rugs on the walls and floor, ornate cushions from the Orient, silver-plated chests piled one on top of the other. And in the very centre, round the fire, sat Shigai-Bai with his family.

Mutton was boiling with a merry hiss in a large pot over the fire and, now and again, the master would taste it to see if it was ready. At the same time, he was stuffing a skin with minced meat, preparing a tasty sausage. Meanwhile his wife was kneading dough for flat cakes, his daughter was busy plucking a plump goose and his workman was singeing a sheep's head over the fire.

'Good evening, my friends!' said Aldar-Kose in a loud voice as he entered.

Shigai-Bai almost jumped out of his skin. In one movement he banged shut the lid of the pot and sat down on top of his sausage; his wife squatted over the dough, his daughter covered the goose with the hem of her skirt, and his workman hid the sheep's head behind his back.

Being obliged to offer his guest a place by the fire, as custom demanded, Shigai-Bai sat Aldar-Kose down and asked him for news of life in the steppe-lands.

[26]

'There is so much that is interesting and so much that is curious in the steppe-lands,' he said, 'that I fear it would take too long to recount it to you.'

'If you cannot tell much, then tell a little,' said Shigai-Bai, his curiosity roused.

'Well, as I was riding this way, I spied a fat snake crawling through the rushes; in truth, it was fatter even than the sausage you sat on as I entered.'

Shigai-Bai pulled a sour face but said nothing. And Aldar-Kose continued.

'Will you believe me, Bai, when I tell you that this snake had a head as large and black as the sheep's head your workman was just now singeing over the fire, then hid behind his back as I came in?'

Again Shigai-Bai pulled a sour face but held his tongue.

'That snake was crawling along,' said Aldar-Kose, 'and hissing like the pot in which your mutton is cooking. So I jumped down from my horse, snatched up a heavy rock and squashed the snake's head as flat as the dough on which your wife is squatting. Such are the wonders of the steppe. If I have lied to you, may Allah deal me the same fate as the goose your daughter has just plucked.'

Shigai-Bai scowled, his face as red as a turkey. Yet not a scrap of food did he offer his guest.

The two men sat talking till late evening – of heroes, of the great khans, of wayward children, of the hated Mongol tribes. And all the while the mutton kept hissing and sizzling in the pot, filling the yurta with delicious smells.

Aldar-Kose had been long on his journey and his empty belly cried out for food; he kept glancing at the pot, his mouth watering and his belly rumbling. Shigai-Bai smiled at his guest's discomfort, saying:

'Boil, my pot, boil for half a year!'

At last Aldar-Kose rose, stretched himself, took off his boots, lay down and said with a yawn:

'Rest, my boots, rest for two years!'

Shigai-Bai, seeing that his guest had no plans to leave that night, was forced to go to bed himself without his supper. The whole family now stretched themselves out upon the floor, leaving the pot of mutton over the dying embers of the fire.

'As soon as Aldar-Kose falls asleep,' Shigai-Bai told himself, 'I'll help myself to some mutton. Why should I go hungry when my meal is ready?'

So the two men struggled to keep awake. Presently, however, the place rang with the snores of the miser, unable to keep his eyes open any longer.

Aldar-Kose rose, took the mutton from the pot, ate his fill, then threw Shigai-Bai's old boots into the pot. Putting back the lid, he lay down again and went to sleep.

After a time Shigai-Bai awoke, looked hard at Aldar-Kose and, thinking him asleep, cautiously roused his wife and daughter.

'Wake up, wake up!' he whispered. 'We shall have our mutton while the visitor sleeps.'

Removing the lid from the pot, he took out his boots and cut them up with his knife. Passing pieces to his wife and daughter, he began to chew the bits of boot – but he could not bite through the leather.

'It's all that good-for-nothing's fault,' said Shigai-Bai to his wife. 'If he had not kept me talking, the mutton would not have grown so tough. Never mind, when he leaves in the morning, we'll cook it again until it's tender. Put the pieces back into the pot.'

Shigai-Bai's wife gathered up the pieces of boot and tipped them back into the pot. That done, Shigai-Bai bade her rake over the fire and bake him some flat cakes from yesterday's dough.

When the cakes were ready, Shigai-Bai thrust them hurriedly under his robes, still hot, lest his guest should wake and notice them. Then, as it was getting light, he went out into the steppe to look at his herds.

No sooner had the miser left than Aldar-Kose hastened after him, calling:

[28]

'Ah, Shigai-Bai, what a good thing I woke in time, or I would have had to leave without thanking you for your hospitality. I must depart today.'

With that, he threw his arms round Shigai-Bai and pressed him so tight the hot cakes burned the miser's belly!

Unable to stand the pain, he cried:

'Oh, oh! I'm burning! My belly's on fire!'

And, snatching the cakes from inside his robes, he snarled:

'Let the dogs eat them!'

'Come now, Shigai-Bai,' said Aldar-Kose, reproaching him. 'How can a Tartar feed his dogs and let his guest go hungry?'

And he seized the flat cakes from Shigai-Bai and devoured them hungrily.

'Your wife makes fine cakes, Shigai-Bai,' said Aldar-Kose, smacking his lips. 'I've not tasted such cakes for many a long day.'

Shigai-Bai scowled but made no reply. Instead he rode off into the steppe.

Returning late in the evening, Shigai-Bai was furious to find the same Aldar-Kose sitting by the fire.

'You said you were leaving,' he shouted.

'I thought better of it,' replied Aldar-Kose with a grin. 'How can I leave such hospitable people, a wife who bakes such delicious cakes?'

Shigai-Bai ground his teeth in anger, though he could not turn away a guest.

Next morning, Shigai-Bai again made ready to ride into the steppe. Before leaving, he whispered to his wife:

'Give me a gourd of kumis to take with me; but mind Aldar-Kose does not see you.'

Shigai-Bai's wife filled a large gourd with fresh milk from their best mares and gave it to her husband. He concealed it quickly under his robe, then left the yurta.

'All will be well this time,' he told himself.

But Aldar-Kose at once ran out and threw his arms round him. So close did he embrace Shigai-Bai that the gourd overturned and spilt the mare's milk down the miser's legs.

He was so angry that he seized the gourd and thrust it into Aldar-Kose's hands, crying:

'Drink it, drink it, for the love of Allah!'

'And so I shall, since you ask me,' replied the other. 'I would not offend you by refusing.'

And he drank his fill of the kumis.

Once again Shigai-Bai rode off hungry and thirsty, while the cunning Aldar-Kose returned to the yurta, chatting gaily to the wife and daughter.

Thus it continued. Aldar-Kose remained at the miser's home for several days and nights. No matter what the mean host did, he could not outwit Aldar-Kose. Like it or not, he was bound to feed and entertain his unwelcome guest.

The miser racked his brains, trying to find a way to rid himself of Aldar-Kose ... And at last he had a plan. Aldar-Kose had ridden on an old grey horse with a white star on its forehead; Shigai-Bai would kill the horse and get his revenge.

But Aldar-Kose noticed the evil glances the miser was giving his horse, and he guessed his wicked thoughts. So that same evening he took some soot and smeared it over the white star on his horse's forehead, while dabbing white clay on the head of Shigai-Bai's best stallion.

That done, he returned to the yurta and went to sleep.

In the still of the night Shigai-Bai stole out of the yurta, found the horse with the white star on its forehead and slit its throat. Then he cried loudly and joyfully:

'Oh dear, oh dear! What a shame for you, Aldar-Kose! Something terrible has befallen your horse. Now what will you do?'

But Aldar-Kose did not stir from his bed. Instead he called back, 'It matters little. Cut up the horse and you and I will have a feast.'

Shigai-Bai leapt up and down with glee, so pleased was he that he had got his revenge on his guest.

In the morning, however, he all but burst with fury when he saw that he had slaughtered his best stallion. But the act was done and there was nothing for it but to cook the meat and share it with Aldar-Kose.

As the days passed, Aldar-Kose wearied of staying with the old miser; and he made up his mind to return to his own aul. However, he would take Shigai-Bai's daughter with him.

'Far better for her to be my wife', he reasoned, 'than to live a miserable life in the home of her father. She would surely become as miserly as he.'

Now, Shigai-Bai's daughter, who was a quiet and gentle girl – Bo-Bulduk by name – had become fond of the carefree Aldar-Kose. Whenever her father's back was turned, she would steal a glance at the handsome stranger.

One morning, as Shigai-Bai was about to ride off into the steppe, Aldar-Kose came to him and said:

'Well, Shigai-Bai, I have stayed with you long enough. It is time for me to leave. When you return this evening, there will be room enough to spare in your home.'

Shigai-Bai could scarcely believe his ears.

'Only give me your bow and some arrows,' Aldar-Kose went on. 'I wish to hunt for food on my way.'

'All right, all right,' grumbled Shigai-Bai. 'Take the bow and arrows and be off with you. It's high time!'

With these words, Shigai-Bai mounted his horse and got ready to ride into the steppe. In the meantime Aldar-Kose ran into the yurta, saying to Shigai-Bai's wife:

'Well, old woman, get your daughter ready; Bo-Bulduk is coming with me.'

'Are you mad?' exclaimed the old woman. 'Do you imagine that Shigai-Bai would give his daughter to a beggar?'

'He has given her to me already. If you don't believe it, ask him yourself.'

[31]

Shigai-Bai's wife rushed from the yurta and called to her husband:
'Shigai-Bai! Shigai-Bai! Is it true? Did you give your Bo to Aldar-Kose?'

'Yes, yes!' called back Shigai-Bai. 'Give him my bow – and let him get out of my home!'

The miser whipped his horse and soon vanished from view.

His wife dared not disobey. She dressed her daughter in the richest finery and led her out to Aldar-Kose. He seated the girl upon his own horse and, taking one of Shigai-Bai's horses for himself, rode off towards his native aul.

That evening, when Shigai-Bai returned home, he learnt what had happened. In a fury, he leaped upon his horse and galloped off in pursuit of the pair. But, though he rode throughout the steppe-lands, he could find no trace of the clever Aldar-Kose or his daughter.

Thus he had to return home to live his miserly life in the solitary yurta in the steppe.

Far, far away, in a small aul, meanwhile, there lived a happy pair, Aldar-Kose and Bo-Bulduk. And never was a husband more loving and gentle than Aldar-Kose to his young wife.

The Nightingale's Song

THERE once lived a merchant who traded in lands beyond the southern winds. And, whenever he returned from a journey, he would bring back some new and costly treasure, so that his house became resplendent with carpets from Persia, silks from China, furs from Turkey and even servants from India.

The merchant also had a nightingale.

The bird lived in a magnificent cage with walls interlaced with silver twigs, the roof lined with crystal-plate and the floor spread with gold dust.

Nothing was too grand for the merchant's dear nightingale. Each day at dawn, midday and sundown, servants would bring crystal-clear water in a mother-of-pearl shell and choice corn on an amber tray.

And what a master of song that bird was – more moving than a sigh plucking at the heartstrings.

'After all, he is far better with me than in freedom,' thought the merchant whenever he heard the song of the nightingale.

One day the merchant was preparing to take his wares to foreign lands; hearing of this, the nightingale made a request.

'Listen, Master. You have always been kind to me; please do me a small favour. You are leaving for my home-land: there you will find my brothers and sisters in a fragrant garden of pomegranate trees. Please go there and tell them I am well and would like a message from them.'

'Very well,' said the merchant, 'I shall do my best.'

And off he went on his travels.

He came to foreign lands, disposed of his wares, purchased all manner of rich and exotic treasure and, when his business was done, he set off in search of the pomegranate garden.

[33]

He journeyed far and wide until at last he came to a garden of rare beauty: the flowers were of a delicate bloom and fragrance; the pomegranate trees were pregnant with fruit; the air about was sweet and trembled with the song of the nightingales. Wherever he looked, there, on every tree, on every branch, sat a nightingale, trilling its song in a clear, flute-like voice.

'Surely this must be the home of my dear songbird,' sighed the merchant. And, going up to a tree, he called:

'Ho, there, Nightingale, your brother lives at home with me in a silver cage. He sends his greetings and wishes you to know he is well, eats his fill, drinks sweetly and wants for nothing.'

On hearing this, the nightingale fell to the ground ... as one dead!

The merchant was perplexed. He bent over the bird and saw that its wings were still, its beak half open; it lay as lifeless as a fallen autumn leaf.

'Oh dear, perhaps I should not have mentioned its brother,' thought the merchant. 'Clearly, it is so envious of his happy life that it has passed clean away... Alas, I can do nothing for it now.'

With that, he picked up the tiny lifeless body and cast it into the long grass.

But, then, no sooner had the nightingale touched the grass than it came to life. It fluttered up to a tree, shook its feathers, chirped and whistled and hopped from branch to branch, from tree to tree, into the very heart of the garden.

'Where are you going? Wait!' cried the merchant in amazement. 'Tell me what message to give your brother. He waits to hear from you ...'

But the nightingale ignored him. Singing gaily, it flew out of sight into the thick shrubbery.

Puzzled and sad, the merchant turned for home.

'Well, Master,' asked the merchant's dear nightingale when he finally returned home, 'did you give greetings to my brothers? Do you have a message from them?'

'I told your brothers all about you,' answered the merchant, 'and I

gave them your greetings; but I have brought no message back. Your brothers would not even listen to me. As I was telling one of them of your happy life with me, it fell down as if dead. And so cleverly – wings still, beak open – you'd never guess it was alive. So I threw it into the long grass. Then, what do you think? Suddenly it came to life and flew off chirping... Did not even thank me for the greetings.'

Hearing this, the poor nightingale began to grieve. All day long he would not eat or drink or sing. And in the morning, when the servants brought his crystal-clear water in the mother-of-pearl shell and his choice corn on an amber tray, the poor nightingale lay dead.

The merchant wept in sorrow.

He tried everything to rouse his dear nightingale: he poured water down his throat; warmed him in the sunshine; laid him on the grass – so great was the merchant's love of his songbird. But it was no use.

The nightingale was dead.

At last, the merchant ordered his servants to take the dead bird from the house and throw his body to the bottom of the garden.

Then, can you guess? The instant that nightingale touched the ground, he came to life, shook his feathers in the sunshine and, singing gaily, soared high above the garden.

'Thank you, Master, for bringing me such good advice!' he cried, winging his way homewards.

The Fern Girl

EARLY one morning a little old woman, mistress of five cows, went out into the fields.

In the first field – which was as wide as the great White River – she found a fern with five shoots. Carefully pulling it up without harming the roots, she took it to her yurta and laid it gently on her pillow.

Then back she went to milk her cows.

As she sat on her milking stool, she caught a faint jingle of bells from inside the yurta. Dropping her milk pail, she ran home as quickly as she could and found a maid of rare and slender beauty sitting on her bed.

It was the Fern Girl!

The little old woman, mistress of five cows, was delighted. She begged the Fern Girl to stay with her and be her daughter. And so it was agreed.

Not long after, a young hunter, Turat, came riding in the forest near the old woman's home. Seeing a grey squirrel, he let fly an arrow and was astonished to see it miss its mark. One after another he shot his arrows – yet never once hit his prey, though squirrels bounded from spruce to birch to larch, right under his nose. In anger, Turat shot his last arrow high into the air . . . and it shot through the opening of the old woman's yurta.

He strode to the tent and shouted:

'Give back my arrow this instant, old woman!'

But no sound came from the tent.

Even more angry, he strode boldly inside. And there before him sat the Fern Girl, her brows as dark as two black sables. Stunned by her beauty, he rushed from the tent, leapt upon his horse and galloped away.

[37]

'O my parents,' he cried on reaching home, 'the little old woman, mistress of five cows, has a most lovely daughter. I have fallen in love with her and dearly want her for my wife.'

At once Turat's father dispatched his other nine sons on nine white horses to the old woman. When they arrived, they saw the girl – and such was her beauty that they were all quite speechless. Eight of the nine held back, while the eldest approached.

'Little old woman, mistress of five cows,' he began, 'we come on behalf of our brother Turat to ask for this maiden's hand.'

'Then you will have to pay dearly for her,' replied the old woman. 'I ask as many cows and horses as my fields will hold.'

Soon a bargain was struck and the cows and horses were driven to their new pastures – more fine steeds than the eye could count. Afterwards the Fern Girl was dressed in finery and given a dappled mare with a silver bridle, a silver saddle and a silver whip. Turat led out his bride, set her upon the dappled horse and rode off home with her.

They had not covered half the journey when a red fox suddenly ran across the track.

Now Turat, being a true jigit, could not resist the chase. So he called to his young bride:

'I shall ride after the fox but will soon be back. Meanwhile follow this road to the crossroads – to the east hangs a sableskin, to the west a white-throated bearskin. Take the turning by the sable; on no account travel westwards.'

With that he rode off in pursuit of the red fox.

The Fern Girl continued on alone and, in due course, came to the crossroads. But by now she had forgotten Turat's words and took the turning by the white-throated bearskin. Riding down this road, she came to a black iron yurta.

And there a most awful fate awaited her.

For out of the yurta, dressed all in black, stepped the Devil's eighth daughter.

A truly horrible sight!

She had but one crooked leg, one arm as crooked as her leg, a hideous dead eye in the centre of her forehead, and a long black tongue that hung down to her breast.

Straightaway the Devil's eighth daughter seized the Fern Girl, dragged her from the dappled mare, stripped the skin from her face and stretched it over her own. Then she pulled off the maid's fine clothes and, donning them herself, flung the girl over the iron yurta. That done, she mounted the dappled mare and rode off to the east.

It was not long before Turat overtook her, just as she was nearing his father's home. Since she was wearing the Fern Girl's skin and clothes, he noticed nothing amiss.

All Turat's brothers and sisters had gathered to welcome the lovely bride; nine handsome youths and eight beautiful maidens advanced to greet her.

Among themselves, the maidens said:

'Do you know, when she opens her mouth to speak the prettiest beads will fall and roll across the ground.'

So they fetched thread to string the beads.

And the handsome youths spoke thus among themselves:

'Do you know, wherever she walks black sables will follow in her footsteps.'

So they took their bows and arrows ready to shoot the sables.

Yet, when the bride spoke, slimy green toads fell from her mouth; and, as she took each step, ugly stoats loped after her.

All Turat's clan drew back aghast.

But, for their brother's sake, they concealed their disgust and, spreading a carpet of green grass before the bride, they led her to the bridegroom's yurta.

All throughout the wedding feast, no one guessed that the bride was not what she seemed.

In the meantime, far, far away from these festivities, the little old woman, mistress of five cows, was going to the field to milk her cows. To her surprise she came upon a new fern with five shoots, just like the first, on the selfsame spot – even more slender and straight than the first.

She carefully pulled up the fern together with its roots, took it home and gently placed it upon her pillow. Then she returned to her milking.

As before, she heard a bell jingling in her yurta. Hurrying back, whom should she find but her dear Fern Girl – even more lovely than before, though very sad.

'Why are you here, my child?' asked the old woman.

'O my mother,' the Fern Girl replied, 'as Turat and I were riding to his aul, he rode after a red fox, telling me to follow the road to the east. But I was unmindful of his words and took the wrong turning – the one by a bearskin. And I came to a black iron yurta.

'There the Devil's eighth daughter met me, clawed the skin from my face and stretched it over her own; she pulled off my fine clothes and, dressing herself in them, threw me over her iron yurta. She then mounted my dappled mare and rode away, leaving me as dead. I would surely be there still had not two grey dogs seized me and dragged me to the pasture near your home.

'And so I grew again as the fern you found. O Mother, will I ever see Turat again?'

'Of course,' exclaimed the old woman, comforting her. 'Meanwhile you shall stay with me and be my daughter as before.'

Thus once more the Fern Girl made her home with the little old woman.

Not long after, the dappled mare heard it from the wind that the Fern Girl was back with the little old woman and spoke about it to Turat's father.

'On the way here your son left his young wife and she was seized by the Devil's eighth daughter. That witch now dwells within your home as your daughter-in-law; soon she will bring misfortune upon you and all your family.'

Hearing this, Turat's father rushed to his son and told him the dappled mare's story.

[40]

'The Devil's eighth daughter has deceived us, my son. Go to the little old woman's place and beg your bride's forgiveness. As for the Devil's daughter, you must tie her to a wild horse's tail and set it loose across the plain! If you do not, she will bring death and misfortune upon us all.'

Turat wept in anguish and anger. He seized the Devil's eighth daughter, dragged her out and bound her to the tail of a wild horse. Then, with a kick and a scream, the horse was driven across the open plain; it trampled upon the Devil's daughter turning her body into a black mass of squirming snakes.

And these Turat and his father gathered up and burned.

That done, Turat set off on the dappled mare to the little old woman's home, where he was greeted by the mistress.

But the Fern Girl wept.

'Why have you come to me?' she asked through her tears. 'You let the Devil's daughter spill my blood and tear my skin; you let my body be seized by two grey dogs. How can you come to me now?'

'I never willingly gave you up to the Devil's daughter,' replied Turat. 'I never willingly gave you to the grey dogs. I would rather have died myself than have you harmed.'

Turat the hunter hung his head, begging forgiveness.

The little old woman, mistress of five cows, seated herself between Turat and the Fern Girl, brushed the tears from the maid's right eye, brushed the tears from her left eye and spoke gently to the girl:

'How is it that you died and came back to us? Were lost and then found? Why do you not rejoice? You must love Turat as before, live in peace and happiness, raise a family...'

The Fern Girl bowed her head, was silent for a time, then spoke softly:

'Very well, I shall do as you say. I shall forgive and try to forget.'

Hearing these words, Turat embraced his beloved bride and together they bade farewell to the little old woman. They saddled the dappled mare, bridled her with a silver bridle, covered her with a silver horse-cloth and hung a silver whip at her side. And the Fern Girl dressed even more splendidly than before. Once more they set out for Turat's aul. The journey was even longer than before.

> *Winter came: they knew it by the snow that fell.*
> *Summer by the warm showers of rain.*
> *Autumn by the mist that enshrouded them.*
> *And spring by the scented feather grass.*

On and on they rode until at last they drew near to Turat's aul.

As soon as they were sighted, a thick carpet of green grass was spread from the tethering post to the yurta.

'When the bride comes,' Turat's brothers said, 'she will walk upon the grass and, wherever she treads, sables will leap from her footprints.'

So they set to making bows and arrows. They worked so hard that the skin was rubbed from the palms of their hands.

Meanwhile Turat's eight sisters set to spinning thread; they toiled so hard the skin peeled off their fingers. As they waited for the bride, they told one another:

'When she comes, she will speak to us in silvery tones, and precious beads will drop from her lips.'

Presently Turat arrived with his bride. Two brothers tied the horses to the tethering post, then helped the bride from her horse to the soft grass.

The Fern Girl spoke words of greeting . . . and red beads fell from her lips. The sisters at once began to gather them up and string them on fine thread.

As the bride walked over the soft grass to the yurta, black sables appeared in her footsteps . . . and the nine brothers took their bows to shoot them.

The Fern Girl entered her new home and, with the crowns of three young larches, herself made up a fire upon the hearth. Soon the yurta rang to the wedding songs of the many guests, who came to greet the happy pair. For three days and nights the feast continued and, when it was over, the guests departed – some on foot, some on horseback.

The Fern Girl

Turat and the lovely Fern Girl raised a family. As the mistress of five cows had said, they lived in peace and happiness for years and years and years.

Some folk say that their grandchildren live on still in the Tartar lands beyond the White River.

How the Bear Lost his Tail and the Bees Gained a Friend

IN ancient times, when the magpie was a Cossack chief and the duck a policeman, the bear had a long bushy tail, as splendid as Mistress Fox's.

Now bear had a fondness for honey. He would spend days just dreaming of getting his paws upon some sweet, sticky honeycomb. No sooner did his sleepy eyes alight upon a bee's nest than he would give a whoop and a jig, climb up that tree, tear out the nest and treat himself to a feast of honey.

Of course the angry bees would try to sting the intruder – but his fur was too long and their sting too short, which suited Master Bear admirably. He would slither down the tree, roll over and over in the moss and crush all the buzzing bees tangled in his coat. Then up he would jump and finish off the remaining honey – with not a bee or a buzz to bother him.

One time, however, a huntsman appeared in those parts and spied Master Bear in a tree, scoffing honey and swatting bees with his long bushy tail.

'Ah, you bow-legged devil,' thought the man. 'I'll climb that tree and chop off your head. That'll put an end to your tricks!'

So he climbed the tree, swung his axe ... swish, swash! But, as the axe came down, the man slipped and, instead of chopping off bear's head – off went his long bushy tail!

What a nasty shock for Master Bear!

He tumbled down from the tree and trundled off home as fast as his stumpy legs would carry him.

[44]

And that is how bear lost his bushy tail. But it is only half our story. For, back in the tree, the huntsman peered into the hollow, set right the nest, put back the honeycomb and went home.

'How peculiar!' thought the bees.

They asked their queen why it was that the man had not eaten their honey, as bear always had? The queen herself did not know. Wishing to find out, she sent her messengers after the huntsman.

'If I were to eat your honey,' he explained, 'what would you have

left for winter? Would you not die of hunger? Then there would be no honey for anyone.'

The messenger bees flew back to the queen with the answer; and she summoned all her subjects to a bee-council which resolved to invite the man to guard bees from the bear. The messengers again flew off.

'Guard us from the rampaging, scavenging bear,' they said. 'Take us to your home and we shall repay you with as much honey as you desire.'

The man agreed.

He made the bees a hive, where they would live in peace from the bear and store their honey.

And, from that time on, the bees have lived in our gardens and given us sweet, delicious honey.

The Tale of the Kurai

LONG, long ago, when some folk were already dead and others not yet born, there lived a khan who summoned young men to shave his head.

But the poor lads never saw their kinsfolk again.

Thus perished the best jigits of the land and people began to wonder how they would save those young men who remained. For no one dared disobey the khan.

Now there dwelt in one aul a humble family with three sons. Presently their turn came to serve the khan; off went the eldest dutifully to the palace ... and did not return.

Months later the second son departed. He too failed to return.

Finally the khan's messengers came for the third and last son, Yamgur.

Since the old father was very poor and had given all he had to the first two sons, nothing remained for the third. But the mother thought of something: she mixed a dough from goose feet moistened with her own milk, and with this she made her son rolls for the journey. With these rolls in his pocket, Yamgur took leave of his parents and set off on his long journey to the khan.

After two sunrises he arrived tired and hungry at the palace. But he was given no time to rest: at once he was brought before the khan, handed a sharp knife and ordered to shave the royal pate. What a shock awaited Yamgur when he uncovered the khan's head!

For there in the centre of his forehead grew a horn, hard and ugly like a wild boar's tusk. The boy tried to hide his horror; he quickly shaved the head and stood back to await his fate.

'I shall have your throat slit,' announced the khan. 'But, before you die, you may make a last request.'

[46]

Since he had not eaten on the journey, Yamgur took out his mother's rolls and began to eat. Seeing the boy greedily devouring these rolls, the khan was curious to try them himself.

Willingly Yamgur handed the fearsome khan a roll. As he ate, the khan smiled his pleasure and demanded to know how such delicious rolls were made.

'Because we are so poor,' explained Yamgur, 'my mother made these rolls with goose feet moistened with her own milk...'

A worried frown wrinkled the khan's newly shaven head.

'I have eaten a roll kneaded in his mother's milk!' he thought. 'Thus, I am now his blood-brother and dare not shed his blood. And yet, should I let him go, he will certainly tell the world of my horned head. What am I to do?'

[47]

At last he made up his mind to banish Yamgur to a forsaken forest where no human had ever been.

So the mighty khan called his attendants and gave them orders. Yamgur was blindfolded, bound hand and foot and borne away across the plain. When they finally arrived at the forsaken forest, the khan's men drove poor Yamgur into the depths of the forest where only wild beasts roamed.

And yet, as time passed, Yamgur did not fall prey to wolves or bears. He kept himself alive, living off the roots and berries of the forest, making himself a bow and arrows to hunt with and, when his clothes were in tatters, he made new garments from hides and furs.

Thus he survived.

Yet all the while he grieved, thinking of his mother and father, his native Irenduk hills, his beloved aul – though unable to escape from his wretched forest home.

One afternoon, he sank down to rest beneath an oak and suddenly heard a strange, yet somehow familiar, sound. Springing to his feet, he followed this mellifluous tune, until he had climbed to the top of a hill. And there he found himself up to his chest in long reedy grass: each blade had a dry hollow stem and bulbous head – like a long trumpet. As it swayed in the wind, this grass gave out a deep, mellow, horn-like sound.

Yamgur quickly broke off a stem, held it up to the wind and blew into it – and heard to his great joy the notes of the now familiar music. Delighted by his discovery, he began to practise each day on the 'kurai', as he called his new instrument. He learnt to play the beloved songs he recalled from his homeland, whatever came into his head. And this music made his heart grow lighter.

Thus it was, playing his kurai, he wandered through the forest and emerged onto an endless plain that stretched to the horizon. After many days he came finally to his native land, though he did not know it yet. As he sat upon a grassy mound playing his kurai, to his great joy he suddenly saw herdsmen running towards him from their near-by grazing ground: they were Yamgur's kinsmen, overjoyed to find their long-lost brother.

When Yamgur was brought down into the valley, he recounted all his adventures to the villagers: how the fearsome khan was killing young people, how he himself had come to live in the forest and how he had saved himself.

So enraged were the people at the khan's cruelty that they formed an army from all the auls around and, with Yamgur at their head, marched against the khan to take their revenge for his tyranny.

Since that time the kurai has been the favourite instrument of the Tartar tribes; you may still hear, echoing through the Ural hills, the very tunes that Yamgur played on his lonely travels through the forsaken forest.

The Cock who Wanted to be Shah

A COCKEREL was strutting about the farmyard one day, preening himself and tossing his red cockscomb; he inspected every nook and cranny of the yard, ensuring that all was ready for his parade.

Satisfied at last, he perched on a high fence and announced to his subjects:

'Cock-a-doodle-do! Cock-a-doodle-do! I am the cock shah, the cock padishah, the cock khan, the cock sultan! Tell me, dear hens, my black and white speckled hens, who is the wisest of all, who is the bravest in the world?'

All the hens came running – the black ones, the white ones, the speckled ones – to pay homage to their great shah, their grand padishah, their gracious khan, their glorious sultan, bustling round him on all sides, squawking:

'Where, oh where, oh where, noble khan? Where, oh where, oh where, mighty sultan? Where, oh where, oh where, gracious shah? Where, oh where, oh where, high and mighty padishah, is there one to compare with you? No one on earth is braver, no one in this world is wiser, no one in God's kingdom is more handsome.'

'Cock-a-doodle-do! Cock-a-doodle-do!' crowed the cock even louder. 'Tell me, dear hens, my black and white and speckled hens, who has a voice louder than thunder? Who has legs faster than the wind? Who has plumage brighter than the sun?'

The hens cackled and gabbled:

'Where, oh where, oh where can the thunder match you? Where, oh where, oh where can the wind match you? Where, oh where, oh where may the sun compare with you? You are our gracious khan, our mighty sultan, our noble shah, our high and mighty padishah!'

[50]

The cock puffed himself up haughtily, drew in his head, shook his red cockscomb and cried at the top of his voice:

'Cock-a-doodle-do! Cock-a-doodle-do! Tell me, my hens, my black and white speckled hens, come closer and tell me more plainly: what khan has a throne higher than all others? What sultan has a crown finer than all others?'

The hens came scuttling right up to the fence, bowed before their glorious sultan, scrabbled and gabbled in a chorus:

'Where, oh where, oh where is there such a khan? Where, oh where, oh where is there such a sultan? You, O gracious shah, high and mighty padishah, you were born with a crown, you will sit forever on a throne.'

Now, listening from his palace to all this babble, the great khan grew very cross and sent guards to seize the cock. They soon caught the boaster and brought him back to the palace.

What a to-do arose in the yard when the cock was taken! The hens all cackled together:

'O woe! O sorrow! Where, oh where, oh where is our gracious khan, our mighty sultan, our noble shah, our royal padishah?'

But the cockerel khan, the chicken sultan was already on the kitchen table with the palace cooks sharpening knives over him and stoking the oven fire.

'Cock-a-doodle-do! Cock-a-doodle-do!' screamed the cock. 'My dear hens, my black and white and speckled hens, the khan has overpowered me, the sultan has conquered me, he has ordered his men to sharpen their knives and stoke the palace fires.'

The cooks cut off the cock's head, boiled him in a great iron pot, placed him on a silver platter and garnished him with boiled rice.

You might well think, Dear Reader, that this put an end to the cock's cackle – well, bless you, and so it should. Yet he was no ordinary bird: would you believe it? Now he crowed even louder than before – not a bit put out by the loss of his head!

'Cock-a-doodle-do! Cock-a-doodle-do! Look at me, I've come from the oven unharmed! I'm lying on a silver platter. See how handsome I look!'

The khan meanwhile prepared to eat the cock, but that bird still shrieked for all he was worth:

'Cock-a-doodle-do! Cock-a-doodle-do! What an honour it is to be eaten with such fine rice!'

Even as the khan carved him up and began to devour him, the cock's voice did not stop:

'Cock-a-doodle-do! Cock-a-doodle-do! How tasty are my bones, to

be sure. Down I go into the khan's stomach. Cock-a-doodle-do! Now my feet are running along little alleyways. My, oh my, it's dark in this chamber; no doors, no windows. Worse than my henhouse!'

The khan finished his supper and lay down to sleep.

But not for long.

Just before daybreak the cock took up his dawn cry from inside the khan's stomach:

'Cock-a-doodle-do!'

Once he crowed, twice ... and the third time, the khan sprang out of bed, crying:

'Cut open my stomach quickly, get that bird out of me! He won't leave me in peace.'

So they opened up the khan's enormously fat stomach ... and out flew the cock, scuttering back to the farmyard.

Onto the fence he hopped and crowed at the top of his voice,

'Cock-a-doodle-do! Cock-a-doodle-do!

'You see, my dear hens, my black and white and speckled hens – nothing can harm me.

> *They cut off my head,*
> *boiled me in an iron pot,*
> *put me on a silver platter,*
> *ground their teeth on my bones,*
> *I slid down the khan's throat,*
> *and landed in his stomach.*
> *Yet here I am safe and sound!*

'Now I'm going to wage war on that dreadful khan and conquer the world...

'Cock-a-doodle-do!'

And off he strutted round the yard to slay flies and grubs and ants and beetles.

Woe

I n ancient times there lived two brothers: one was very rich, the other poor. The rich brother had gone to the city, built himself a fine mansion and become known far and wide as a merchant of repute.

The other brother had remained in the village and was so poor he had not even a scrap of bread to bait his fish hooks.

One day he made up his mind to visit his wealthy brother: he walked all the way to the city, sought out his brother's house and told him how things were.

'Help me, Brother,' he begged. 'Give me any work so that I may earn a crust of bread for my wife and children.'

'All right,' replied the rich brother, 'I'll hire you for a week, then we'll see what you're worth.'

For a whole week the poor man toiled like a slave and, in payment, received a loaf of bread.

That pleased him greatly and, with a word of thanks, he prepared to leave for home.

But his brother called him back,

'Not so fast! Tomorrow is my birthday – bring your wife to my party.'

The poor man mumbled his thanks, but on the road home he thought:

'How can I dine in such company? I have nothing to wear; my last cloak has more holes than a fishing net...'

All the same he did not wish to offend his brother.

'Tomorrow is my brother's birthday,' he told his wife on reaching home. 'He has invited us to his party.'

'Then let us go since we are invited,' said his wife.

The next day they set off together for the city and, arriving at the brother's house, they bowed humbly and took their seats at a rickety table in one shadowy corner of the hall. The guests came, all well-to-do and showy, each congratulating the host. And he, in turn, paid them all respectful compliments and was most attentive to their needs.

Yet he paid not the slightest attention to his brother; nor did the servants bring them any food or drink. They sat uncomfortably in the corner, went hungry and finally left unnoticed.

On the way home, the poor man said to his wife:

'I have a mind to sing.'

His wife was surprised.

'In Allah's name, what for? Folk sing when they are happy – what have you to sing about?'

'Folk will hear me,' he replied, 'and say "that rich brother treated him so well he's singing with joy".'

'Then go ahead and sing if you want.'

So the poor man struck up a song, a tune as doleful as it was cheerless. His lone voice penetrated the gloom of evening; yet presently he heard a second voice, as joyless and tuneless as his own. Much surprised he turned to his wife.

'Is that you singing in that reedy voice, Woman?'

His wife shook her head.

Once more the poor man took up his song. Immediately another trembling voice joined in.

'I wonder whether that is Woe accompanying me?' he said aloud.

'It is I,' answered Woe, in a flat, bass voice.

'Well, what is to be done? Aida ... aida, come home with us. You and I travel the same road,' said the poor man.

So the three continued the journey together: the poor man, his wife and Woe. Once home, Woe said to the poor man:

'Let's drown our sorrows in a little drink.'

'But I've no money,' he objected.

Woe would not leave him be.

'Sell your cloak. It won't last till summer anyway.'

[55]

The poor man sold his cloak and they drank on the proceeds. The next morning both had sore heads.

'Let's try a hair of the dog that's bitten us,' suggested Woe.

The poor man turned out his pockets – not a button.

'Don't worry,' said Woe nonchalantly. 'Take your sled and ox-cart and sell them. We'll drink on that.'

The sled and ox-cart were sold and the money spent on more drink. Again their heads were sore.

'Don't worry,' Woe comforted the poor man. 'Fetch your plough and rake and sell them.'

Again they drank and again their heads spun. And so it continued until the poor man had sold every last thing he ever owned.

'Let's have another drink,' said Woe.

'You do as you wish,' replied the poor man, 'but I've nothing left to drink with.'

Seeing the man was telling the truth, Woe bade him borrow horses and a cart from his neighbour. That done, they harnessed the horses to the cart and jogged off into the forest.

They had not gone far when Woe said:

'Drive the cart over to that big rock.'

As they reached the rock, Woe jumped down and ordered the poor man to help him move the rock. But it was very heavy. Eventually they just managed to shift it a few paces. When the poor man looked, his mouth dropped open in amazement ... for the hole was filled to the top with gold coins.

'Don't stand there gawping,' said Woe. 'Load the gold onto the cart.'

Soon the cart was full and the hole empty. However, the poor man set to thinking:

'If Woe comes home with me, I'll be ruined again in no time at all.'

So he resorted to cunning.

'What's that glittering at the bottom of the hole?' he asked.

'I don't see anything; it must be your imagination.'

But the poor man insisted:

'If you don't believe me, climb down and see for yourself.'

No sooner had Woe climbed into the hole than the poor man heaved the rock back over it. Then he drove on home.

With all this treasure, he soon paid his debts, bought himself fine clothes and built a grand dwelling. Then he hired a pair of horses, drove to the city, and brought his wealthy brother home to supper.

Seeing how his brother now lived, the rich man was quite envious and even more astonished when he heard the story.

And he made up his mind to find that rock for himself.

Having taken his leave, he rode off like the wind, found the rock and tried to shift it. After much pushing and straining, he finally moved it to one side – and out leaped Woe, who sprang upon him and clung tightly to his back.

'So, my friend,' yelled Woe, 'you did not wish to share the fortune with me; you intended to leave me in the hole! Now you will never lose me.'

The wealthy brother tried to explain.

'Don't be angry with me. It was all my brother's fault. I came to rescue you.'

'Don't lie to save your miserable skin,' said Woe half-mad with rage. 'You tricked me once, but not again!'

And he stuck like pitch to the rich man's back. From that time on, wherever the rich brother went, Woe went too, clinging to his back and drinking his fortune away.

The Wolf and the Tailor

A TAILOR was coming along a forest path when he found himself face to face with a wolf ...

Seeing no escape, he spoke up boldly:

'Ah, my dear wolf, I see you desire to eat me up. It is not my wish to deny you your dinner; only please permit me one last request.

'Being a tailor, I take pride in my trade and wish to take your measurements – length and width – so that I might fit snugly inside you.'

The hungry wolf wanted to devour the tailor at once; but he mastered his greed and gave his consent.

Thereupon the tailor took an iron rule from his bag and, holding the wolf firmly by the tail, he hit him ... whack! ... hard on his head with the rule – so hard the wolf fell senseless to the ground.

And the tailor made good his escape.

When the wolf came to his senses, he cursed his stupidity.

'Why did I agree to be measured? For sure, I could have eaten the tailor at more than one sitting...'

With these sad ruminations, the wolf slunk away, still hungry and just a jot wiser than before.

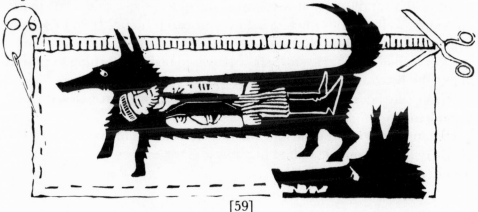

Shaitan the Devil and his Forty Daughters

THERE once lived a man, Safa by name, who tired of his dull life and decided to see the world. So he bade farewell to his wife and family and set off in search of adventure.

Whether he was long in his search I cannot tell you, but one day he arrived at the shores of a great lake just in time to see a beautiful white swan fall into the clutches of a black witch. However much the swan screeched and flapped its wings, it could not tear itself free.

Without a thought to himself, Safa dashed forward with a loud shout, putting the witch to flight. Of course the swan was more grateful than words can tell; he had saved its life and now it would reward him.

'Beyond this lake, beyond the seven hills,' it said, 'live my sisters. Sit upon my back and we shall fly to them.'

Safa sat astride the white swan and off they flew over the lake and the seven hills until they came to the swan's sisters – who were overjoyed to welcome the man who had saved their dear sister. They treated him most kindly, gave him honey and kumis and presented him with a small box.

'Take this small token as a reward,' the eldest sister said. 'But mark my words well: do not open it before you reach home. If you do, you will regret it most bitterly.'

After he had left the sisters, Safa was overcome by a burning curiosity about the box; and it grew stronger and stronger.

'What can be in this box that I must not open it on my way?' he wondered.

He journeyed on and on but, in the end, he could not contain his curiosity any longer; he halted in a forest glade and opened the box . . .

Glory be to Allah!

In an instant there appeared in the glade a market stall selling ribbons and jade, cushions and carpets, jewels and porcelain. And from every side came merchants hurrying to the stall, bargaining for the merchandise and paying Safa good coin. Soon he had so much money that he had nowhere to put it all!

At first he was overjoyed at the stall and the wares and the money. But he could hardly stand forever trading in the forest. And when he tried to shut the box, he could not. More and more merchants arrived and more and more money poured through his hands. Finally he sank to his knees, cursing himself for disobeying the white swan. Why had he opened the box before reaching home?

Even as he cursed his weakness, from out of nowhere appeared an old, old man with a long grey beard.

'Why do you grieve so, my son?' he asked Safa.

Safa explained.

'Perhaps I can help you,' said the old grey-beard. 'But I make one condition: you must give me what you have at home about which you know nothing.'

Safa was puzzled: what could he have at home about which he knew nothing? Though he pondered long and hard, he could think of no answer to the riddle.

'All right,' he said. 'I shall give you that of which you speak. Only do help me quickly.'

'Mind your promise,' warned the old man.

With these words, the old man shut the lid of the box ... and all the trinkets and jade, the merchants and money, the stall and all the wares disappeared inside.

Thankfully Safa took up his box and continued on his way; he had wanted to thank the old grey-beard, but the man had vanished as though the earth had swallowed him up.

In truth the old man was none other than Shaitan the Devil! And the promise he had extracted from Safa was one he would bitterly regret.

When Safa arrived home, his wife met him joyfully; for, while Safa

[61]

had been on his journey, his wife had borne him a son – a strong and handsome lad, the image of his bold father. At once Safa realized what he had done: with tears of anguish, he told his wife of the vow he had made to the old man in the forest.

Yet, as the years went by, and the boy grew up, they forgot the pact with the Devil ... until one day old grey-beard appeared before Safa.

'Remember your vow, Safa,' he said. 'It's time for you to part with your son.'

Next day Safa told his son about the magic box, of the old man and of his promise.

'Never mind, Ata,' said his son. 'Since you've given your word you must keep it.'

So the youthful jigit took leave of his father and mother and went on his way to keep the appointment with the Devil. When he reached the lakeside, he sat down on a rock to await his fate. All of a sudden he heard a fluttering of wings above him, and down to the lake flew a flock of white swans. Not noticing the young man, they settled on the water and began to frisk and play in the shallows near the shore. Thinking of catching one of these graceful birds, the jigit crept towards them and seized one in his strong arms; at once the other birds flew off in alarm, leaving behind their poor trapped sister – the youngest and most graceful of the swans.

To the jigit's surprise, the swan addressed him in a human voice,

'Please let me go; if you do I shall help you.'

She shook her wings and turned into a beautiful maiden. Addressing the jigit once more, she said:

'I am the youngest daughter of Shaitan to whom your father made his vow. My father lives on human flesh and means to eat you; but you can be saved if you obey my words. The moment Shaitan goes to eat you, ask at once for some work...'

With that the lovely swan girl waved her graceful arms and soared up to the heavens.

No sooner was she out of sight than the terrible Shaitan himself appeared at the lakeside to claim his victim. Seeing the jigit, he snatched him up and carried him off to his palace in the depths of the forest. He was about to devour him when the boy, recalling the swan girl's advice, spoke up boldly:

'Give me some work to do; I'm not ready to be eaten yet.'

'All right,' said Shaitan grudgingly. 'I'll give you work: you shall chop down this forest in one night and arrange logs in bundles ready for sale. When you've sold them all, buy rye with the money and sow it on the cleared ground. That same night, you must gather in the harvest, grind the corn and store the hay in my barn. If you fail, you will be eaten immediately!'

Shaitan left the jigit wondering how he would set about his impossible task. However, towards evening he was visited by the swan girl, daughter of Shaitan. Hearing of the task her father had set, she said:

'Do not grieve, my friend; I'll see to it myself. Meanwhile lie down and sleep soundly till morning.'

As soon as the jigit was asleep, the swan girl went out onto the porch and whistled softly; at her call all the jinns of the forest gathered about her ready to do her bidding.

To each the girl gave orders and it was not long before all the work was done – exactly as her father had commanded. The instant the cocks began to crow the jinns scattered as if they had never been.

When the sun was already up, Shaitan arrived and saw to his amazement that all was indeed done as he had ordered.

'Clearly this is no ordinary mortal!' he thought. And, addressing the boy, he said, 'You have passed your first test. Now you shall have a second: in one night you must carry the water from one lake to another in a sieve!'

As soon as Shaitan had gone the swan girl appeared and asked what it was her father had asked. When she learned of the new task, she again summoned all the jinns of the forest and gave each his orders to fetch the water. The sun had not yet risen when all the water had been taken from one lake to another; the cocks crowed and the jinns vanished – the work complete.

Shaitan was amazed and very angry. But he now thought of something the lad could never do: bridle and tame a certain stallion from his stables.

'Should you succeed in this impossible task,' he said, 'you shall wed my youngest daughter.'

Once the Devil had gone, the jigit hurried to meet the swan girl and tell her of his new task.

'This is much harder,' she said. 'My father will turn himself into that untamed stallion. But there is one way you may bridle him: first you must get the blacksmith to make you a forty-ton iron lash and the tanner to make you a forty-ton leather bridle.'

When the hammer lash and the leather bridle were ready, the jigit went to the stables and found the untamed stallion of which Shaitan had spoken. Sparks and fire poured from his nostrils, his mane shook like an angry sea and he pounded the ground with his hoofs, letting no one near him.

Keeping out of reach of the stamping hoofs, the jigit quickly darted forward and dealt the stallion a sharp blow with his forty-ton lash. That quietened the steed who no longer kicked his hoofs or tossed his mane. In an instant the jigit had fitted the forty-ton bridle and led him from the stables.

As the jigit sprang upon his back and gave both flanks the heavy lash, the stallion raced forward bucking and twisting, snorting and rearing, trying to throw his rider to the ground and trample upon him. But, no matter what he did, the jigit clung on and would not be unseated.

After a long battle, the stallion had to submit and returned tamely to the stables. The jigit dismounted, locked the stable doors and went to the swan girl to tell her of his success.

'Tomorrow', she said, 'my father will turn his forty daughters into doves and will ask you to pick me out from among them. You should point to the one that flies nearest to you.'

On the morrow, as she had said, Shaitan called the jigit to him and pointed to a flock of doves.

'You see those doves,' he said; 'among them is my youngest daughter. If you can pick her out, you will be saved and you may take her as your wife.'

Straining his eyes, the jigit would certainly not have known had not a small white dove flown close to his head. At once he cried:

'There is your youngest daughter! The small white dove.'

Shaitan flew into a rage, guessing that his daughter had told the jigit how to recognize her. Not keeping to the bargain, Shaitan prepared another test for his daughter's hand.

That evening the youngest daughter came to the jigit and told him:

'Tomorrow morning my father will again ask you to find me among my sisters. We shall be playing the kurai for you to dance. And, when my sisters stop to watch you, I shall continue the tune – that is how you will recognize me.'

And so it was; the next day Shaitan called the jigit to him and pointed to his forty daughters.

'Should you pick out my youngest daughter,' he said, 'you shall take her as your wife. But should you fail, then you will pay with your life.'

The forty maidens were all dressed exactly alike and each held a kurai. At a sign from their father, they put the instruments to their lips and began to play.

'Well, jigit,' said Shaitan, 'which of these girls is my youngest daughter?'

But the jigit did not answer; instead he began to dance to the exciting music. All the girls stopped and stared in admiration as he whirled about them – all, that is, save one who continued to play. Stealing a glance at the solitary player, the young jigit continued his dancing and, when the music finally stopped, he went up to the girl and announced triumphantly:

'This is Shaitan's youngest daughter!'

[65]

'You couldn't know that by yourself!' shouted Shaitan in a rage. 'She must have helped you. Now I shall teach you both a lesson!'

Immediately he gave orders for the jigit and his youngest daughter to be thrown into the dungeon. But the daughter was again too smart for her father: during the night she changed herself into a fly and flew out of the dungeon. Then, turning back into a young girl, she ran to the threshing floor and, gathering up two sheaves of corn, took them back to the dungeon. The guard had dozed off and did not notice her bringing the strange bundles into the cell.

Placing the sheaves on the floor of the cell, she covered them with her cloak and spat upon the pile.

'Now, dear friend,' she said, 'we must linger here no longer; it is time for us to flee.'

This time she turned both the jigit and herself into flies and together they flew from the dungeon into the fresh night; then, taking their former shapes, they hastened to make good their escape.

Next day at dawn the executioner went down to the cell to waken the prisoners. Seeing the bundles lying on the dungeon floor, he shouted:

'Hey you! Are you still asleep?'

'Yes, we are still sleeping!' answered the spit on top of the sheaves of corn.

'I shall soon be taking the heads off your shoulders!' called the executioner.

'Yes, we know that well,' came back the voice.

Thus the conversation went for as long as the spit upon the sheaves stayed moist. The executioner kept putting his questions until, after a time, he got no reply – the spit had all dried up.

'What, fallen asleep again, have you?' he shouted. 'Then I'll have to wake you up!'

With these words, he opened the cell door, entered the dungeon and gave the bundle of clothes such a blow with his axe that pieces of hay flew everywhere – making him cough and sneeze. It was only then that he realized he had been tricked! Rushing to Shaitan, he informed him

[67]

that the prisoners had escaped, leaving the two sheaves of corn in their place.

Shaitan was furious; at once he sent his men in pursuit of the fleeing pair. By this time, however, the girl and the jigit had put a great distance between themselves and the palace. But Shaitan's men were soon hard on their heels. Hearing the thunder of horses' hoofs behind her, the girl said:

'Shaitan's men are almost upon us; quick, we must hide!'

And she turned herself into a mosque and the jigit into an old muezzin; so that, when the riders came up, they bowed respectfully and asked the old muezzin:

'Have you seen a girl and a jigit pass this way?'

'No,' replied the muezzin. 'Many years have I served in this mosque, and never have I set eyes on a girl and a jigit.'

Shaitan's men returned to the palace empty-handed and told their master they had come upon nobody but an old muezzin in a mosque. Shaitan fell upon his men in a fury, cursing them for their stupidity.

'Camel dung!' he fumed. 'That muezzin and the mosque were the fugitives you were after! Ride back as fast as the wind, seize that muezzin and smash the mosque.'

But, when the riders arrived at the spot on which the mosque had stood, they discovered no mosque and no muezzin. So they galloped on. The girl and the jigit had taken their former shapes and hurried on their way. As soon as the girl heard the thunder of hoofs, she cried:

'Shaitan's men are behind us once again; quick, we must hide!'

This time she turned the jigit into a shepherd and herself into a flock of sheep; so that, when the men rode up, they were again deceived.

'Hey there, shepherd,' they shouted. 'Did you see a girl and a jigit pass this way?'

'I've tended my flocks here for many years,' replied the old shepherd, 'but I've never set eyes on the girl and young man of whom you speak. They have not passed this way, I assure you.'

Once more the riders had to return unsuccessful to their master. This time they reported that they had met no one but an old shepherd tending a flock of sheep. Shaitan was even more angry than before and cursed his men more violently. Then he jumped upon his steed and set off himself in pursuit of the fleeing pair.

By this time the girl and the jigit had taken their former shapes and were running on; but Shaitan was soon on their heels and would surely have caught them had the girl not heard him and realized the danger they were in. In a flash she turned herself into a sea and the jigit into a golden fish. And, as Shaitan rode up to the sea, he cried in triumph:

'I've got you now! You won't escape me this time!'

Plunging into the water, he began to swim after the golden fish. But he did not catch the fish. Neither did he catch his daughter. For the sea dragged him down and down and down ... and drowned him.

Afterwards the girl and the jigit changed back into human form and rode on Shaitan's steed to the jigit's native aul. How happy his mother and father were to greet their son and his young bride-to-be. Soon they were wed and lived a long life of peace and harmony.

The Boy with the Golden Knucklebones

ONE day, when an old Tartar went down to the Great Lake to water his horses, he was surprised to see them shy away from the lake, toss their heads and paw the ground. Evidently an evil spirit was snatching at their manes and stopping them from drinking.

'What can it be?' he asked himself. 'I had better try the water myself.'

No sooner did he bend down to drink than – Allah save us! – someone was clutching at his beard! However hard he wriggled and tugged, he could not break free.

A hideous face took shape in the water – with long green whiskers that flowed back over its shoulders like reins, great bloodshot eyes and four yellow teeth that were as sharp and hooked as those of a walrus.

In horror the old man recognized the face at once: it was none other than Ubyr, the most fearsome of all the witches.

'Let me go, Ubyr!' the old man shrieked. 'I'll gladly give you my flock of sheep.'

'I don't want your sheep,' Ubyr snarled.

'My herd of horses, then.'

'I don't want your horses.'

'What will you take?'

'Nothing more than that of which you have but one,' said the witch mysteriously.

In his confusion the old man did not stop to think.

'Very well,' he agreed hurriedly. 'You shall have it – only let me go.'

When Ubyr released him, he ran off as fast as he could, with the witch's words ringing in his ears,

'Mind you keep your word ... Nobody can hide from me!'

The old man hurried home, and then suddenly he realized what he had promised to Ubyr. His only son, Altyn-Saka! Saying nothing of this to his wife and son, he made haste to lead his family far from the lake.

On the first day in their new home, Altyn-Saka missed his knucklebones and became very miserable. He had got the name Altyn-Saka – Golden Knucklebones – because he played knucklebones better than all the other children. And now his knucklebones were gone.

'We must have left them behind in our old home,' said his father. 'Only you must not go there, for Ubyr will surely catch you.'

And he confessed to his son all that had happened at the lake.

Altyn-Saka listened to his father's story, but said:

'I do not fear Ubyr, father. She will not catch me; I'll return to you. Only give me a horse that is fleet of foot.'

The old man pleaded with him not to go, but the lad was stubborn: he wanted his lucky knucklebones and that was that! Finally the old man gave in.

'Very well, be it as you wish. Go to my herd, swing your whip high above your head and take whichever steed comes first to you.'

Altyn-Saka went to the herd, swung his whip, rattled his bridle and at once a scraggy colt came limping towards him.

'I shall have to take this scraggy colt, it seems,' he said gloomily, mindful of his father's words.

However, as soon as he touched the colt's neck with his whip, its tangled coat fell away to reveal a strong, sleek body. And, as he led the horse from the pasture, it grew into a tall and stately stallion. Then it spoke:

'Ubyr awaits you at the lakeside. She will tell you to dismount and pick up your knucklebones. But you must not obey her. For, if you do, she will gobble you up in the wink of an eye. You must be as swift as a hawk, bend down quickly and snatch up your knucklebones.'

Altyn-Saka leapt upon the stallion and rode off to the lakeside, where he found Ubyr sitting at a fire warming her hands.

'Greetings, Grannie,' he said, 'I have come for my lucky knucklebones.'

'Then pick them up, my lad,' Ubyr replied. 'My poor back aches and I cannot hand them to you.'

Swift as lightning, Altyn-Saka's horse bent its head low so that its master could snatch up his knucklebones – and galloped on its way. Ubyr jumped up with a howl of rage. She spat once – and an enormous black stallion appeared beside her. She spat again – and black reins appeared. Then up she sprang upon the horse and sped off in pursuit of Altyn-Saka.

Fast as the wind, the two horses raced over the plain. But the witch's horse was steadily overtaking the other and soon drew level; Ubyr was about to seize Altyn-Saka when her enormous black stallion stumbled and dropped behind.

So furious was the witch that she ate up the horse and had to run along on foot after the lad. Faster and faster she ran, urging herself on by punching and pinching herself; again she caught up with the stallion and bit through its right hind leg. Yet the horse galloped even faster on three legs. Once more Ubyr overtook the stallion and this time bit through its left hind leg. Though badly hurt, the stallion mustered its remaining strength and dashed on, bearing Altyn-Saka away from Ubyr. But its strength was giving out and, as they reached a lake, it said:

'I cannot run any more; I'll hide from Ubyr in the lake until my wounds heal. Meanwhile you must climb that oak yonder and shelter in its branches.'

And straight into the water plunged the stallion while Altyn-Saka quickly climbed the oak-tree and hid in its branches.

But Ubyr was as keen-sighted as she was fleet of foot. As she ran up, she at once spied the lad hiding in the topmost branches of the tree.

'I have you now!' she screamed. 'I'll chop down this tree and gobble you up in no time at all!'

She spat once – and an axe appeared.

Then she pulled out a tooth and, whetting her axe upon it, she set to hacking down the oak, the chips flying to all sides as she worked.

All this rumpus brought a fox running to the scene.

'Why are you chopping down this tree, Grandmother?' it asked.

'Do you not see, stupid animal,' cried Ubyr, 'I am chopping it down to get at Altyn-Saka.'

Looking up, the fox noticed the young lad trembling in the tree, and it took pity on him.

'You are old, Ubyr,' said the fox. 'Let me chop down the oak for you. Then you'll be fresh to eat him.'

Ubyr thankfully agreed and handed the fox her axe; she lay down to rest beneath the tree and fell asleep at once. As she slept, sparks and smoke poured from her nostrils!

While Ubyr slumbered on, the fox threw the axe and Ubyr's whet-stone-tooth into the lake, then gathered up all the chips, fitted them back into the tree, spat on them, licked them and . . . the tree at once became whole.

Thereupon, with a cheery wave to Altyn-Saka, the fox dashed off into the bushes.

However, before the lad had time to clamber down from the tree, the witch had woken up.

'What's this I see!' she stormed. 'The oak is whole again as though I had never touched it!'

Cursing the fox and its cunning tricks, Ubyr once again spat, took an axe out of thin air, pulled another tooth from her mouth and began whetting the axe. All the while she chopped, she kept glancing up at Altyn-Saka, calling:

'I shall chop down this tree and gobble you up in the wink of an eye!'

The chips flew to all sides and soon the oak shook and trembled. Another hard stroke and it would surely topple.

Just at that moment another fox ran up.

'What are you doing, Grandmother?' it asked of Ubyr.

'Chopping down this tree so that I can eat Altyn-Saka,' the witch replied.

'Don't tire yourself,' said the fox. 'I'll chop down the tree for you.'

'No, no!' grumbled the witch. 'I can manage myself. Just now there was another fox here and he promised to help me; instead I was tricked.'

'What colour was that fox?' asked the second fox.

'Red.'

'Never trust a red fox, Grandmother,' it retorted. 'Red foxes are cheats, all of them. You can only trust black foxes.'

Ubyr looked and saw that, indeed, the second fox was as black as a raven's wing. So, with a thankful sigh, she gave in, handed over the axe and lay down to rest. Once again the smoke and sparks poured from her nostrils as she slept.

Meantime the black fox hurled Ubyr's axe and whetstone-tooth into the lake, fitted the chips back into the cut, spat upon them, licked them and – well I never! – they grew fast and the oak became whole again.

With a flick of its bushy tail, the black fox vanished from sight.

But, before Altyn-Saka could make good his escape, Ubyr awoke and flew into a rage. Seeing the tree whole again, she spat in a rage – and an axe appeared. She pulled a third tooth from her mouth and whet the axe. Then she hacked and hewed, cursing all foxes with the most poisonous names she could think of.

It was not long before the tree was cut halfway through; and poor Altyn-Saka began to tremble.

Suddenly, as if from nowhere, a grey fox ran up and called to Ubyr:

'Let me help you cut down the tree, Grandmother.'

'Be off with you,' screamed the witch. 'Twice already foxes have fooled me and run away.'

'But what colour were they?' asked the third fox.

'One was red, the other black,' Ubyr replied.

'Never trust red or black foxes, Grandmother,' said the grey fox. 'They are terrible liars and cheats. You can only trust grey foxes.'

Seeing that the fox was grey, Ubyr entrusted the axe to it and settled down to sleep before dealing with Altyn-Saka. Meanwhile the grey fox threw the axe and the third tooth into the lake and, quickly gathering up the chips, fitted them back into the tree.

Then it spat on them, licked them and ... the tree became whole once more.

Turning to Altyn-Saka, the fox said:

'Thrice I have come to your aid: I smeared my fur with black pitch and then with grey clay so as to fool Ubyr. But there is nothing more I can do for you.'

Bidding Altyn-Saka farewell, the fox raced away.

Once again, before Altyn-Saka could escape, Ubyr awoke in a towering rage.

'What's this I see!' she screamed. 'I've been tricked a third time. But I won't be tricked again.'

Thereupon she spat into the air, took down an axe, pulled out her last remaining tooth, whet the axe and, when it was razor sharp, started to chop down the tree.

The chips flew to all sides, the oak creaked and groaned and seemed about to come crashing down.

Altyn-Saka thought his end was near.

Just at that moment a raven alighted on a branch beside him.

'Save me, Raven,' he pleaded. 'Fly quickly to my home, find my two faithful dogs, Akkulak and Aktyrnak, and bid them come quickly; I need their help.'

But the raven shook its head.

'Why should I help you? When Ubyr has killed you and chewed on your bones, I shall have the remains.'

And the raven settled down to wait.

Presently, a magpie flew down.

'Listen, Magpie,' begged Altyn-Saka. 'Fly to my home and fetch my two dogs, Akkulak and Aktyrnak; I need their help.'

But the magpie shook its head.

'Why should I?' it replied. 'When Ubyr has killed you and eaten your flesh, I shall pick your bones.'

Altyn-Saka was desperate. Yet, just as he had given up hope, a flock of little sparrows flew overhead.

'Hear me, little grey sparrows,' he called. 'Fly to my home, tell my trusty dogs, Akkulak and Aktyrnak, that the old witch is about to eat their master.'

'We shall find them! We shall find them!' chattered the sparrows cheerfully; and away they flew to Altyn-Saka's home.

When they arrived, the birds found the two dogs fast asleep; so they pecked at their ears to try and waken them. Then the sparrows set up a great chirruping and fluttering.

'Come Akkulak, come Aktyrnak,' they called. 'Hurry to the big oak that grows by the lake and save your master. Ubyr is about to eat him.'

Straightaway the two dogs sprang up and raced to the lake, kicking up clouds of dust as they ran. When Ubyr saw the dust-clouds she became alarmed and asked Altyn-Saka what it meant.

'They bring joy to me and woe to you,' the jigit replied.

At that instant, Akkulak and Aktyrnak ran up, rushed at Ubyr and chased her into the lake. The dogs called to their master:

'We shall dive into the waters after the witch; watch the lake carefully.

'If Ubyr kills us – the water will turn red.

'If we kill her – the water will turn black.'

With these words, the two dogs plunged into the water of the lake.

At once the water began to seethe and boil. And, as Altyn-Saka looked on anxiously, it started to turn red . . .

'Ubyr has slain my dogs,' he said in anguish.

Yet even as he looked – Allah be praised! – the water turned black! Altyn-Saka was overjoyed. Climbing down from the tree, he ran to greet his two dogs shaking off the black water as they came.

'Tell me, my faithful friends,' he said, 'why did the water of the lake first turn red?'

Akkulak replied:

'Because Ubyr was getting the better of us; she even bit off one of my ears. But we soon made short work of her and left her dead at the bottom of the lake.'

The handsome stallion had followed the dogs out of the lake.

[77]

'Come, Altyn-Saka,' it said, 'jump upon my back and I shall carry you home to your father.'

And when Altyn-Saka arrived home, a great feast was held to celebrate: it lasted full nine days and nine nights and is still remembered by Tartar folk to mark the end of the terrible Ubyr.

A Tartar Riddle: Which is Biggest?

WHEN he died, an old peasant left his three sons a white bull to share amongst them. How were they to divide the bull into three?

First they thought of selling him and sharing the money. But they found no one in the neighbourhood rich enough to pay their price. Then they thought of killing the bull and dividing up his meat. Yet they felt sorry for the beast and decided against it.

Since none of them would give the bull up to the others, they had to go finally to the khan for advice.

So off they set for the Court on the other side of the valley.

The eldest brother walked by the bull's head, the second at the bull's side and the third behind, driving him along with a stick.

At dawn the youngest brother was overtaken by a horseman who asked where he was heading.

'We are taking our bull to the khan to settle a dispute for us,' said the lad. And he added, 'As you ride across the valley, you will overtake my second brother by the bull's side. Give him my greetings and tell him to urge on the bull. We must arrive by nightfall.'

'Very well,' called the rider.

At noon, he caught up with the second brother.

'Your brother sends greetings,' he said, 'and asks you to urge on the bull if you wish to arrive before dusk.'

The second brother thanked the horseman and said:

'When you reach the bull's head, give my greetings to my eldest brother and tell him to drive the bull faster. We must reach the khan before dark.'

The horseman rode on, but it was evening by the time he reached the bull's head and passed on the second brother's message.

[79]

'There is nothing I can do,' said the eldest brother. 'It is already dusk. We must halt soon and spend the night by the roadside.'

The horseman rode on.

Meanwhile the brothers spent the night in the open valley. And the following morning they started out again, driving the white bull farther.

All of a sudden a huge eagle swooped down, seized the bull in its talons and flew off into the clouds.

The brothers grieved and sorrowed and returned home empty-handed.

In the meantime the eagle soared on through the clouds with the white bull; but it soon grew weary and, seeing a goatherd with his flock of goats below, dropped down to rest upon the horns of the largest goat. And there it began to eat the bull and strew his bones to all sides.

As the eagle was having its meal, the heavens opened and rain descended, sending the goatherd and his flock to shelter beneath the beard of the goat that supported the eagle.

Yet, as the goatherd sheltered from the rain, he felt a sharp pain in his eye.

'A speck of dust,' he thought. 'I must return to the village and see a doctor.'

By the time he reached the village, the pain in his eye had grown worse and he cried out to the villagers:

'Call in forty doctors, my friends. Let them sail in forty ships round my eye and find that mote. It gives me not a moment's peace.'

So the villagers found forty doctors and gave them the goatherd's message. Thus the forty doctors in their forty ships set sail in the goatherd's eye; and they found the mote that was not a mote but the bladebone of the white bull. It had entered the goatherd's eye as he was sheltering under the goat's beard.

The moment the bladebone was removed, the eye healed, the doctors went home and the bull's bone was taken beyond the village and cast away.

[80]

Some time later wandering nomads were passing the spot where the bladebone lay. Not recognizing it for what it was, they made camp and built a fire right next to the bone's resting place.

'This salt marsh is the safest place for us to spend the night,' the nomads said.

However, just as they were settling down to sleep, the ground began to tremble and shake, scaring them so much they hurriedly piled their belongings into their carts, hitched up their horses and moved off in great haste.

Only when the first rays of dawn appeared did they recover from the fright and send riders back to discover what had happened. When the riders arrived at the salt marsh, they saw that it was not a salt marsh at all but a huge bone – the bladebone of the white bull – at which a red fox was now gnawing.

'So that is what made the ground tremble and shake,' the riders cried. Thereupon they took out their bows and shot the fox, killing it on the spot. At once they set to skinning it where it lay but, try as they might, the men could not turn the fox over to skin the other side. In the end they had to leave it half-skinned.

They then rode back to the rest of the nomads and told the strange story. As they displayed the fox fur, a young woman approached and addressed the men:

'I want to make a cap for my baby; may I have a piece of your fur?'

The nomads were only too eager to give her all the fur they had. The woman then measured her baby's head and began cutting a cap for him out of the fox's skin. But it wasn't long before she saw there was enough only to make half a cap; so she went to the nomads for the second half of the skin.

The riders confessed they had been unable to turn the fox over to skin the other side.

'If you cannot make your baby a cap from one half of the fox's fur,' they told her, 'you had better go and skin the fox yourself.'

A Tartar Riddle: Which is Biggest?

That the woman did: with no effort at all, she lifted the fox, skinned its second side and made her baby a cap from the two halves of the fur.

And that is where our strange tale ends...

*

But here is the riddle: which was the biggest of them all?

Was it the white bull?

After all, it took a man on horseback a whole day to ride from his tail to his head.

Or was it the eagle?

After all, the eagle carried the white bull in its talons through the clouds.

Or was it the goat with the long horns?

Do not forget, it was on its horns that the eagle perched while devouring the bull.

Was it the goatherd?

It took forty doctors to sail in forty ships round his eye.

Or could it be the fox?

After all, it was the fox that started the earthquake by gnawing the bull's bladebone.

Was it the baby?

It took the entire fox's skin to make him a cap...

Or was it the woman who had such a giant for a baby?

Think hard, think long. And perhaps you will find the answer to this riddle.

The Tale of the Three Talismans

LONG, long ago, when there was less noise and more green on the broad banks of Lake Baikal, a poor peasant lived in an aul beside the lake.

One day, when his three sons were crying for food, he borrowed a hunting gun from his neighbour and went off into the forest. Pushing his way through the bracken, he emerged after a time into a clearing where there stood a most peculiar tree, all gnarled and broad-armed. On a branch of that tree sat a big bird just as misshapen as the tree. Thinking of his starving sons, the peasant took aim and fired and down tumbled the bird at his feet.

And then a strange thing happened.

Just as he was about to pick up the bird, it opened its orange beak and spoke in a human voice:

'Do not slay me, Hunter. Spare me and I shall help you.'

So saying, it took a neatly folded cloth from under its wing and presented it to the hunter.

'This cloth is a talisman to bring you luck,' it said. 'If you desire food, you have only to wave this cloth and you shall have whatever nourishment your heart desires; should you want drink, the magic cloth will provide meads and kumis to slake your thirst.'

The poor peasant was amazed and overjoyed; he took the cloth and set free the bird.

As soon as he reached home, he waved the cloth before his sons and, in the twinkling of an eye, the floor was spread with all manner of tasty viands and meads. So from that time on the poor peasant and his sons never lacked for food.

Some months later a great khan was passing by the lake on his return from hunting in the hills. Being hungry, he sent scouts to find a house

[83]

where he might dine; and they soon heard about the poor peasant. So the khan paid a visit to the owner of the magic cloth.

As soon as the khan was seated in the place of honour, all kinds of dishes were laid before him; even the great khan had never set eyes on such rich and tasty food. He suspected sorcery in the way such food appeared out of thin air. But he could not guess the secret.

When the khan returned to his palace, he was informed that envoys were on their way from Stambul – from the Great Ruler of the Faithful himself. At once the khan dispatched messengers to the poor peasant summoning him to the palace to entertain the sultan's envoys.

Naturally the peasant could not refuse. So he called his eldest son, Osman, handed him the magic cloth and bade him take good care of it in the khan's palace. Osman came before the khan, promised to prepare a grand feast but, following his father's instructions, asked to be left alone in the banqueting hall – where no one would witness his preparations.

Eager to please the sultan's envoys, the khan consented and ordered his servants to take Osman to the grand hall. A short time before the visitors were due, however, the khan himself went to see whether the banquet was ready. How outraged he was to find Osman reclining upon the cushions and not a morsel in sight!

'Is nothing ready, son of a pig?' he cried in a rage. 'By the beard of my father! I shall have you thrown from the tallest minaret, boiled in oil and dragged across the plains!'

'Pray spare yourself the pains, O Mighty Khan,' replied Osman coolly. 'All will be ready for your visitors.'

The moment the khan had gone, Osman waved the magic cloth and, in a trice, the floor was richly spread with the most exotic dishes. Naturally, on his return, the khan was delighted, and he marvelled at the short time Osman had taken to prepare them, though he guessed the boy had used some sort of magic.

Being eager to gain possession of the secret, he showered favours upon the boy, saying:

'Such a clever jigit should marry my only daughter, the Princess Isharad.'

Osman was overwhelmed by such blandishments. The very next day the wedding was celebrated and the khan's daughter became the wife of Osman, the poor peasant's son. Of course Osman was not to know that the crafty khan had instructed his daughter to learn the secret of the magic cloth and steal it from her new husband.

That evening the Princess Isharad stroked and teased Osman, saying:

'Tell me, O heaven-sent Husband, by what charms and powers did you prepare such a feast?'

'With nought save this simple cloth,' answered Osman innocently, taking the cloth from under his coat.

The moment Princess Isharad saw the cloth, she snatched it up and ran to her father.

'Cast him into the dungeons, behind the door with seven locks!' commanded the khan, pleased at the success of his scheme.

Thus it was that the poor peasant came to lose his eldest son and the magic cloth.

Time passed and the old peasant found himself again in such want that he had nothing to give his starving sons. Once more he borrowed his neighbour's gun and went to the forest. And again he came upon that strange misshapen bird on a branch of that gnarled and sprawling tree in the centre of that selfsame clearing.

Bang! He fired at the bird, knocking it from its perch; as it landed at his feet, it said:

'Do not kill me, Hunter. Take this purse and, when you are in need, shake it ... gold coins will shower from it.'

The old man was overjoyed at this new magic and hurried home with it. Showing it to his two sons, he shook it hard and, to their joy, gold pieces showered upon the cottage floor.

With such a fortune the old peasant soon built himself a new home — such as was not to be found in that aul or the next or, indeed, in Bakchiserai itself.

[85]

But he was not left to enjoy his wealth for long. Once again the khan passed by the lake on his return from hunting. At the sight of the old man's new abode, the khan blinked in astonishment, suspecting more sorcery.

For sure the khan could not be outdone: he sent his men to the old peasant, summoning him to the Court so that he might build the khan a new and magnificent palace.

On receiving this order, the old peasant sent his second son Mustafa to the Court. Entrusting him with the magic purse, he bade him take good care of it and to return once his mission was over.

Mustafa was taken before the khan to receive his instructions. Yet, as he ventured to inquire about payment for the new palace, the khan exclaimed:

'Your father has a dwelling more costly than my own, yet he possesses no great fortune. Build my palace free – or I shall have you hurled from the palace cupola!'

So Mustafa set to building the palace for the khan, and paid for everything forthwith in good gold coin. When the magnificent building was complete, the khan came to him.

'Such a valorous jigit is worthy of my only daughter,' he began. 'You shall be my son and heir and have the new palace for your home.'

Mustafa was quite enchanted by such flattery; and that same day the wedding took place between the khan's daughter and the peasant's second son.

In the evening the Princess Isharad carried out her father's instructions, caressing Mustafa and whispering to him:

'O heaven-sent Husband! What unknown charms have made you so rich and powerful? Unfold to me, your humble slave, the secret of your fortune.'

Unsuspecting, Mustafa drew out the purse from under his coat and showed it to his wife. The moment the artful princess set eyes on the purse, she snatched it up and clapped her hands. At once guards came

running in, seized poor Mustafa and threw him into the dungeon, behind the door with seven locks.

Now the old peasant had lost two of his sons, his magic cloth and his wonderful purse. It was not long before hunger once again drove him to take his neighbour's gun and go with his remaining son, Taz-Oglan, into the forest.

The two men wandered about the forest for several days; but this time it seemed their luck was out. In despair and on the point of returning home, they somehow found themselves standing before the unusual tree in the magic glade. Great was the old man's joy to see the orange-beaked bird still in the tree, sitting quietly on a branch.

As before, he fired at the bird which fell at his feet.

'Do not slay me, Hunter,' it implored him. 'Spare me and I shall help you.'

This time the old man received a golden bow.

'You have but to loose an arrow from this golden bow,' said the bird, 'and the arrow will fly to its target fast and true.'

Truth to tell, the old man was not so delighted with this gift, but he returned home with it all the same. On the way back the two men shot so much game with the bow that they could scarcely carry it all. And from that time on their table never lacked for food: they had only to let fly an arrow from the golden bow and down dropped a snipe, pheasant or even a goose.

Not long after the khan was out hunting and came to the lakeside aul. As was the custom in the khan's hunt, all the best local archers were recruited to the party – so the old peasant had to go. During the hunt the khan noticed that the old man brought down all the game he shot at with his golden bow. Once more his suspicions were aroused.

Shortly after this the khan prepared for battle against his enemies. He gathered his army and, remembering the peasant with the golden bow, sent a captain to conscript him.

'How can an old man like me go to war?' he complained. 'Better take my last remaining son, Taz-Oglan.'

So Taz-Oglan marched off to war bearing his father's golden bow. At the first battle, the khan had Taz-Oglan posted at his side so that he could keep an eye on him and his golden bow. Thus it was that the boy stood at the head of the army alongside the mighty khan.

The battle was quickly won, for Taz-Oglan's arrows winged their way to the breast of every foe. On the eve of the next battle the young archer addressed the mighty khan,

'Most glorious of glorious warriors! Permit me to fight the foe alone. I shall put them all to flight with my trusty bow.'

With the khan's consent, Taz-Oglan marched off by himself, met the enemy host on the battlefield and shouted his challenge. The enemy soldiers shook with laughter: one boy against a whole army! Yet no sooner had he shot his arrows into the air than the greater part of the enemy army soon lay slain: each arrow had killed a thousand men!

Now that Taz-Oglan had defeated a whole army, the khan was certain he possessed some sorcery. Thus he praised and flattered the young archer and pledged to him his only daughter.

So Taz-Oglan was married to the lovely Princess Isharad; and in the evening his new wife talked sweetly to him:

'Tell me, O brave warrior, whence came your power to destroy the entire army of our enemy? What talisman guides your arm that you can slay a thousand men with one arrow?'

When Taz-Oglan told her of his golden bow, she begged to see it.

'That is no business of a princess,' he said sternly and went to bed, placing the golden bow beneath his pillow.

But the khan's cunning daughter had put a handkerchief heavy with scent upon the pillow. Taz-Oglan fell into a deep slumber and, as soon as his eyes had closed, she took the magic bow from under his pillow and bore it triumphantly to her father.

As soon as Taz-Oglan awoke, he found himself alone: both his wife and the golden bow were missing. Quickly realizing he had been tricked and was in great danger, he sprang from the bed, slipped past the palace

[89]

guards and ran off to the forest. He was even afraid to show himself in his native aul.

When the old peasant heard that the khan now had the magic bow, and thinking that Taz-Oglan too had met an untimely death, he quickly pined away and soon died.

Many were the dangers that Taz-Oglan had to face in the forest; yet he survived by eating berries and nuts – whatever he could find. When winter came and there was no more food to be found, he grew thin and haggard and would surely have perished had he not come upon that very same tree at which his father had received the three talismans. Despite the barrenness of winter, the tree was as green as in the midst of summer, and it bore delicious fruit rather like ripe figs. In his hunger the boy climbed the tree, picked several of the strange-looking figs and ate them ravenously.

Yet, even as he swallowed them, he felt a peculiar sensation – and he felt horns growing on his head! Two big horns like those of a goat!

The poor boy tried to shake them off, but they were fixed firmly, as much a part of him as his nose and ears. In great anguish he dashed through the forest, knocking against bushes and tree-stumps, trying to rid himself of the unsightly horns. As he rushed madly on, he brushed against the leaves of a tall uncommon bush – and one horn fell off. With a great sigh of relief, he plucked several leaves from the bush and hastily rubbed the other horn with them: immediately the second horn fell from his forehead.

Taz-Oglan realized he had stumbled upon some strange forest magic, which he could turn to his advantage. He collected a basketful of the ripe figs and plucked the leaves of the tall bush. Then, taking the figs and leaves with him, he made his way to the palace gates.

Having lived so long in the forest, he looked for all the world like a tattered beggar, with his straggly beard and ragged attire.

At the palace gates he began to shout his wares:

'Fresh figs for sale! Fresh figs for sale!'

[90]

As soon as the khan's daughter heard that fresh figs were being sold in the midst of winter, she sent a maid to purchase the whole basketful – just as Taz-Oglan wanted. Having sold his basket, he vanished from sight.

The Princess Isharad regaled her father and his courtiers with the ripe figs; each person at Court ate four figs and smacked his lips at the delicious fruit. However, a great commotion soon disturbed the palace – all who had tasted the figs found four ugly horns sprouting from their heads!

Although the khan summoned all the doctors of the realm, not one was found who could rid the royal household of the horrible horns. In despair the khan made it known that he would grant half his empire to the person who could cure him, his daughter and all his courtiers of their terrible malady.

When Taz-Oglan had news of the proclamation, he made his way to the palace and was straightaway admitted to the khan's presence. Taking a leaf from under his robe, he rubbed it on one of the khan's horns – and the horn clattered to the floor. How relieved and delighted the khan was! He was ready to give this beggar any reward. But the healer said:

'I can cure you and all your Court of these accursed horns; yet I do not cherish half your khanate, nor do I want your daughter's hand. My request is quite modest.'

'Your request shall be granted whatever it may be,' said the khan, eager to rid himself of the remaining horns.

'Then return to me my golden bow!' demanded Taz-Oglan, stepping back and throwing off his ragged cloak.

It was only then that the khan recognized the beggar. But, however furious he was, there was nothing he could do: the bow was brought and handed to Taz-Oglan.

'And now,' he said, 'give back the purse and cloth you took from my brothers. Make haste before I fire my bow and kill you all!'

As he drew back the string of his deadly bow, the khan and all the

courtiers fell down in terror – and the princess rushed to bring the talismans.

Taz-Oglan took the three talismans and went to the dungeon where his brothers were imprisoned. Loosing an arrow at the seven locks, he split them asunder and threw open the door – setting free his two brothers and all the other captives who had been locked away by the cruel khan.

'Here are your talismans, my Brothers,' he said. 'Now let us deal with the khan.'

And Taz-Oglan mounted the khan's throne and began to rule the land firmly and justly, his two brothers serving as his viziers. As for the old khan and his daughter and all the courtiers, they were left to run about the Court, shaking their horns and bleating like goats.

Two Lazy Brothers

LONG before you and I were born, there lived two lazy brothers. One day they were strolling through the woods when they came upon an apple-tree. And upon that tree hung the most delicious, juicy apples just waiting to be eaten.

Since the lazy pair were always hungry, one said to the other:

'I say, Brother, let's shake the tree and bring down some apples.'

'I've an even better idea,' said the other. 'Let's lie beneath the tree and let an apple fall into our mouths.'

So they lay on the ground under the apple-tree, their mouths open.

Some moments went by, and one turned to the other:

'Listen, if an apple falls,' he said, 'we shall have to chew it.'

'I didn't think of that,' said the other.

So they got up and went home hungry...

Saran and Yumart

THIS tale goes back to a time long ago when sheep grazed peacefully in the green folds of the Tartar homelands.

In an aul on a hillside lived two neighbours – Saran the miser and Yumart the kind. One day they set out together to seek greener pastures for their sheep. After travelling throughout the first day, by evening they felt hungry so they stopped to rest and take a bite.

Yumart untied his bag, took out some rolls and began to eat. Saran, meantime, fumbled with the neck of his knapsack and finally said to his companion:

'I must have tied this bag too tightly; let's share your rolls today and have mine tomorrow.'

'I don't mind,' replied Yumart. 'Here, help yourself.'

So they had their supper and went to sleep. The next morning they journeyed on. The way was long and dusty, and it was not quite dusk before they again felt hungry.

'Let's eat your rolls now we've started them,' said the miser.

'As you wish,' his companion replied.

So they ate Yumart's rolls on the second day – and on the third day too. Saran showed no sign of untying his knapsack.

On the fourth day, when Yumart's bag was already empty, Saran thought to himself:

'Now he'll want to eat my rolls...'

And, being very mean, the miser stole away in the night while his companion slept. Of course, when Yumart awoke, the miser was nowhere to be seen and both Yumart's bag and his stomach were empty.

He trudged on alone across the plain until he reached a forest. And after walking several hours through the forest he came at last to a tumble-

[95]

down, deserted cottage. Inside, on the shelf, however, stood a loaf of
white bread. Rejoicing at his good fortune, Yumart broke the loaf in
two, ate one half and left the other on the shelf, then lay down behind
the stove to sleep.

Just as his eyes were closing, the door opened and in came a bear,
a fox and a mouse. At once they took the remains of the bread, divided
the half-loaf into three, devoured it hungrily and began to talk.

'Do you know that in this cottage, on top of the stove,' began the
mouse, 'is a pot of silver. When I jump down from the stove you can
hear the coins jingling.'

'And do you know the old oak that grows by our house?' said the
fox. 'Well, under it I've hidden a pile of silver in a sheep's skull. I dug
a hole so deep that no one will ever find it.'

'That's nothing,' said the bear. 'I know of a store of gold that's concealed in a horse's skull along the forest path by a giant lime-tree.'

And so the conversation went on deep into the night before the three friends fell asleep. Early next morning they left the cottage, each about his separate business. The moment they were gone, Yumart crept out, looked around and soon discovered the pot of silver on the stove.

Putting it in his bag, he made for the old oak that stood near the house. There he dug up the sheep's skull full of shining silver coins buried beneath the tree. Next, with the potful of coins and the skull of silver in his bag, he made his way down the forest track until he came to the giant lime – and he set to digging. It was not long before he dug up the horse's skull filled with pieces of gold. Putting this, too, into his bag, he continued his journey through the forest.

It was getting dark by now and he was not sure which way to go. But he had an idea: he would climb a tall tree to spy out the edge of the forest.

Climbing to the topmost branches of a tall fir, he was scanning the forest when he heard a strange noise in the clearing below. Looking down, he saw to his amazement that a host of jinns had gathered beneath the fir and were boasting of their day's exploits. When their chief had heard them out, he asked:

'Where is the blind jinn among you? Bring him forward.'

Hurriedly the blind jinn was thrust forward.

'Why are you so late?' the chief jinn asked.

'Because I was putting a spell on the khan's daughter,' he replied. 'I've given her a sickness that no human can cure.'

'Then tell us the cure,' said the chief.

'In the khan's herd there is a white cow,' answered the blind jinn. 'Were he to slaughter that cow and give its meat to all the townspeople, his daughter would regain her health. But he will never do that because he is very mean.'

As soon as the first rays of dawn pierced the trees, the jinns scampered off; Yumart shinned down the tree and set out for the town that he had

[97]

spied beyond the forest. As he reached the outskirts, he entered a house, saying to the master:

'I am a traveller from afar; what is your news?'

'My friend,' said the host, 'our news is cheerless: the khan's only daughter has fallen gravely ill. So distressed is her father that he has pledged half his khanate to the person who can cure his beloved daughter.'

'Then I shall go to the khan and cure her,' announced Yumart.

Purchasing a thick, musty book at the market – the better to be taken for a wise man – Yumart made his way to the palace.

'I am a healer,' he told the guards. 'Take me to the khan.'

When he had gained an audience, he opened his thick book and read out remedies for the various ailments. Finally, he looked up:

'Ah! Great Khan, you have a white cow among your herds. Have it slaughtered and its meat given to the townspeople. Only then will your daughter be cured.'

Though it did not please the khan to waste his best cow on the towns-folk, he gave the order and the job was done. And that same day the khan's beloved daughter rose from her bed as right as rain. True to his word, the khan granted Yumart half his khanate.

Thus it was that Yumart became a man of considerable means in the town. Soon afterwards he opened a workshop, where artisans taught the children of townsfolk a great variety of skills and trades.

Time passed and then one day, after many travels, Saran the miser found his way to the town. You can imagine his surprise when he learnt that his old companion was now a man of some renown; he sought out Yumart and asked how he had come by such a fortune.

Being a trusting soul, Yumart recounted all his adventures – every-thing that had happened since the day Saran had deserted him. Natur-ally Saran grew very envious. And, as soon as he had left Yumart, he hurried off to find the tumbledown cottage in the depths of the forest.

Following Yumart's directions, Saran soon found the cottage, went in and looked around. Nobody was home, but on the shelf stood a loaf of white bread. So mean and greedy was Saran that he gobbled the entire loaf and went to sleep behind the stove.

Late that evening the owners of the cottage came home: the mouse, the fox and the bear. They at once looked for their bread on the shelf.

'Where is our loaf of bread?' shouted the bear.

'Someone has taken it!' said the fox.

'Perhaps he's still here,' squeaked the mouse.

Said the bear:

'Mouse, you look in all the corners of the cottage and see who is hiding here.'

So the mouse scampered round, peered into the stove – no one there. Next he jumped on top of the stove, then sprang down – right onto the head of the sleeping Saran. The miser woke with a start and jumped out from behind the stove.

'There's the thief that stole our bread!' roared the bear.

In a trice the three animals set upon Saran and tore him to pieces.

Truth to tell, he had only himself to blame; he should not have been so greedy, should he?

Abzelil and the Master of the Lake

In a Tartar aul there lived an old couple who were very poor: they had neither sheep, nor horses, nor goats, not even a hive of bees to give them honey. By and by they died, leaving their son Abzelil only a handful of birch bast.

Abzelil took this down to the great lake, dipped it into the water and set to plaiting the wet bast into a long rope. While he was busy at his task, the fearsome Master of the Lake rose from the watery depths and stood before him. Though he was very frightened, Abzelil contrived to hide his fear.

'What are you doing here, jigit?' the green-bearded ogre cried.

'I am plaiting a rope, as you see,' the lad calmly replied. 'When it is ready, I'm going to hang your lake from the clouds.'

This unexpected reply put fear into the Master.

'No, no, jigit!' he cried. 'Don't touch my lake, I beg of you! I'll grant any wish if only you leave my waters in peace.'

Abzelil paused in his work. What should he ask of the ogre? Since these parts were famous for the fine horses that watered at the great lake, he made up his mind.

'Give me your finest steed,' he said, 'and I'll not touch your lake.'

'Oh no! Those steeds are my fame and strength,' cried the ogre. 'I cannot grant that wish.'

'As you please,' replied Abzelil, 'then I shall have to hang your lake.'

And he continued plaiting his bast rope.

The Master of the Lake was silent.

'Well, bold jigit,' he sighed at last, 'if you are strong enough to hang my waters, then you would surely not refuse a test of strength between

[100]

us first. Come, we'll race round the lake – if you overtake me, I'll grant your wish.'

'Agreed,' said Abzelil. 'There's just one thing: I have a younger brother; if you can beat him first, then I'll compete against you.'

'Where is this brother?' asked the ogre.

'He's sleeping in the bushes,' replied the lad. 'Go yonder and shake him and he'll come running straightaway.'

The ogre went into the bushes at the edge of the lake and out scampered a frightened hare. At once the Master of the Lake gave chase, thinking this was indeed the jigit's younger brother. But he could not catch the hare no matter how fast he ran.

'I'll beat you yet,' he shouted in a rage. 'Let's try our strength at fighting.'

Abzelil agreed.

'But first you must beat my grandfather – he is eighty-eight. If you can knock him off his feet, I shall leave the lake to you. He is over yonder, resting in the hollow; he's a mighty sleeper so you'll have to give him a good crack over the head to rouse him.'

Off went the ogre to the hollow, where a big brown bear was dozing; he gave him a fair crack over the head with a big stick, which did not please the bear. Leaping up, the bear seized the Master of the Lake in his strong arms and threw him crashing to the ground.

Limping back to Abzelil, the old ogre cried:

'How strong your grandfather is! I've no strength left to fight you. But give me one last chance: I have a mare as tall as sixty hands. Let's see which one of us can carry her round the lake.'

'All right,' consented the lad. 'Only you try first.'

The Master lifted the mare on his shoulders and staggered with her round the lake. With a triumphant shout, he set her down before Abzelil.

'So, jigit, now it's your turn.'

Abzelil put aside his rope, went up to the huge horse and said to the ogre scornfully:

'You're not so strong after all! You lifted the mare on your shoulders – just watch me carry her with my feet!'

Thereupon he mounted the horse, dug his heels into her flanks and rode round the lake with ease.

The ogre saw he was beaten. Leading out his best mare, he gave her to Abzelil. And what a fine horse she was: with thick forelock, short mane, narrow croup, tall withers, sharp ears, coppery eyes, hollow cheeks and pointed muzzle.

Abzelil mounted this handsome mare and galloped home.

Folk say that, from then on, fine horses have always watered at the great lake and that the jigits thereabouts are all as bold as Abzelil.

The Three Daughters

In the reign of the Munificent Khan there lived a humble widow. She, poor woman, worked very hard to feed and clothe her three daughters.

As the years passed, the three girls grew up as swift as swallows, with faces as bright and round as the harvest moon. And, one after the other, they married and went their separate ways.

After a time the old mother fell sick and lay on the verge of death in her lonely cottage. With her fading strength, she called her favourite red squirrel and sent it with a message to each daughter.

'Tell them to make haste, my little friend, lest I should die before they come.'

Off scampered the red squirrel to do her bidding. Coming to the eldest daughter, it at once gave the news of her ailing mother.

'Ai-yai-yai!' she moaned. 'I would gladly go at once, but alas! I must stay to clean these bowls.'

'If you cannot go straightaway to your sick mother,' said the red squirrel crossly, 'then stay forever with your bowls!'

With that, the bowls suddenly sprang from the sink, seized the eldest daughter above and below and stuck fast to her; she clattered to the floor and crawled from the house as a tortoise!

Presently the squirrel came to the house of the second daughter. Again it delivered the message.

'Ai-yai-yai!' she sighed. 'Gladly would I go at once if only I weren't so busy. But, as you see, I must weave this cloth for the fair...'

'Then weave on and never stop!' said the red squirrel.

And the second daughter was turned into a spider.

When the messenger came to the house of the youngest daughter, she was kneading dough. The moment she heard the news, she rushed from the house and ran all the way to her mother – without even stopping to wipe her hands. The red squirrel was very pleased.

'Always bring sweetness and joy to people, my child,' it said, 'and they will always love you and your children and your children's children.'

Indeed the youngest daughter lived many long years and was loved by all. And, when her time finally came, she turned into a busy, golden bee.

All day long throughout the summer the bee gathers pollen to make honey, bringing people sweetness and contentment. And in winter, when all around are dying from cold, the little bee sleeps in its hive. As soon as it wakes, it gathers pollen to make more sweet honey and bring joy once more into people's lives.

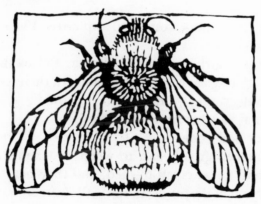

Altynchech and the Padishah's Wife

In the old, old, half-forgotten times, before the gardens of Tartary were overrun with weeds, there lived an old man with his wife and their three lovely daughters.

But after a while the old woman fell sick and died and the widower took another wife for company. The new wife despised her three step-daughters and nagged her husband night and day:

'Take your daughters off, I cannot abide them,' she would say. 'I'll leave you if you don't get rid of them.'

When she had quite poisoned his mind, she sent him off to the forest where he set to digging a pit – very deep and very wide. This he covered with twigs and leaves and returned home, telling the three girls:

'Tomorrow, my daughters, we shall go to the forest to pick berries.'

So, early next morning, the girls happily took their baskets and, suspecting nothing, went with their father to the forest. And while they were busy picking berries their father crept away and shouted from a distance:

'Come quickly; see what a wonderful apple-tree I've found. The fruit is so ripe and juicy.'

Hand in hand, the girls ran to their father. But as they reached the apple-tree the twigs and leaves gave way beneath their feet, and all three plunged into the deep pit. Vainly they cried out:

'Help us, Father, save us from this hole!'

But their father had gone.

The poor frightened girls began to weep, not knowing what to do. But at last they had no tears left to shed, and they bent all their efforts on trying to climb out of the pit. Alas, the walls were smooth and slippery,

there was nothing to cling to and the hole was so deep. Again they set up a loud wailing:

'We cannot get out; we shall die in this hole!'

For three days and nights they sat at the bottom of the hole, eating only the apples that dropped from the tree. And, when the fruit no longer fell, the girls made balls of clay and knocked down apples with them. It was not long before they had brought down every apple from the tree.

How would they survive now? In despair the two eldest girls groaned:

'We shall never get out; it is our fate to remain here forever.' And they resigned themselves to die.

Only the youngest did not give in; after much thinking she led her eldest sister to one side and said:

[107]

'Stand here against the side, Sister. Our second sister will stand on your shoulders, then I'll stand on her shoulders – since I am the lightest. I'll pull myself out by the roots of the tree.'

The two sisters did as she said, while she climbed up on their shoulders and, seizing a root of the apple-tree, pulled herself out of the hole. Without wasting a moment, she gathered an apronful of apples and dropped them down to her sisters, calling:

'Eat the apples and be patient. I'll bring help.'

To her good fortune she soon came upon a hunting party led by the padishah himself. And, when he had heard her story, he straightaway sent four strong men to the pit to help the girls out.

When the girls were rescued and brought before him, the padishah asked the eldest what she could do.

'With a single thread', she replied, 'I can weave linen to clothe an entire regiment.'

'I would clearly like to see such artistry,' said the padishah. And he had a needle and thread brought in.

In next to no time the girl had woven garments for the whole of the padishah's army. Amazed at such skill, he turned to the second sister and asked what she could do.

'With a single loaf of bread', she said, 'I can feed your entire army.'

At once a loaf was brought and the girl divided it to provide an ample portion for every soldier in the army.

The padishah was even more astonished; then he turned to the youngest sister and asked her what she could do.

'I can bear you a son and a daughter', she said, 'fairer than the sky at dawn.'

Pleased by her grace and the promise of a son, the padishah wed the youngest sister and began to live with her in his palace, while he had a grand mansion built for the two sisters beyond the palace walls.

The eldest sisters were jealous.

'How is our sister better than us?' they said. 'Why should she be the padishah's wife?'

Their envy gave them no peace: they plotted to get rid of their sister and take her place in the palace. A chance soon presented itself when the padishah had to go off to war.

'I shall be at war a whole year,' he told his wife. 'Guard the palace well till my return.'

A few months later the youngest sister gave birth to a son and a daughter fairer than the sky at dawn. Everyone who saw the babies stared and marvelled, saying:

'The padishah must be informed at once.'

And so an envoy was sent with the following message:

'You have a wonderful son and a daughter fairer than the sky at dawn.'

Since his journey was long, the envoy made a halt to refresh himself at the mansion of the two sisters. Of course they made him welcome and heated the bath-house.

'You are tired and dusty,' they said, 'and the way ahead is long. Steam yourself in our bath-house to give you strength, then continue your journey refreshed.'

As the envoy was steaming himself, the two sisters took the letter from his pocket, tore it to shreds and wrote another, which said:

'Your wife has borne you two skunks blacker than the sky at night.'

They then resealed the letter and put it back in the envoy's pocket. When the man had washed and dressed, he went unsuspecting on his way.

As soon as he was gone, the two jealous sisters hurried to the palace and, finding their sister asleep, stole her babies and put two black skunks in their place. The babies were taken into the depths of the forest to an old hermit woman's hut.

'Keep these children here with you,' they said. 'Never let them out of your sight and never show them to a living soul!'

Now listen, Dear Friend, to what happened when the padishah learnt from the false letter that his wife had borne him two skunks blacker than the sky at night.

Not wasting a moment, he left the war and hastened home. When he saw that there really were two black skunks in the royal cot, he became frenzied with grief and fury and banished his wife from his sight.

'Build a hut by the wayside,' he shouted to the guards, 'and take this sorceress there with her skunks. Put up a sign so that every passer-by stops and spits upon her!'

When the two wicked sisters learnt of this, they were, of course, delighted. They were even more pleased shortly after, when they were invited to live at the palace.

'Now it is our turn to live in comfort,' they said, 'just like our sister. Let her now sit and sorrow in her wayside hut!'

Thus the years passed. The son and the daughter, fairest of the fair, grew up in the hermit woman's hut in the depths of the forest. The boy grew to manhood, became a skilful hunter and brought back fox and hare and mink and sable for his sister. When, one day, the two wicked sisters arrived to see how the children were faring, they were quite alarmed at how the young boy had grown into a strong and handsome jigit.

'If that boy finds out what we did to his mother,' said the eldest sister, 'he will surely tell the padishah and we shall lose our heads!'

So they thought up a plan. Summoning the old hermit, they told her:

'Put a spell on the girl, then tell this to her brother: "Fetch the wild black stallion for your sister; as soon as she gazes upon that steed she will recover her strength. Without it she will die." Little will he know that the stallion is untamable and has already killed many jigits.'

The hermit woman did as instructed: she worked such a cruel spell on the girl that her brother would do anything to save her.

'Go and fetch the black stallion,' she said, 'show it to your sister and she will get better; otherwise she will die for sure.'

At once he dashed off to seek the black stallion; but not far along the forest track he met an old man who, on hearing of the boy's mission, shook his head and said gloomily:

'You go to your death, my son. That black stallion has already killed many bold jigits.'

[110]

Seeing the boy was determined to go on, the old man handed him a silken lash.

'As the stallion gallops towards you, whip it with this silken lash and seize its mane. But, should you fail, it will kill you for certain.'

The jigit took the lash, thanked the old man for his counsel and continued on his way. On and on he went through the forest until, at last, he came to a green meadow where the untamable steed was grazing. The instant it caught sight of the lad, it reared up and rushed madly at him – meaning to trample him underfoot. But the jigit skilfully dodged aside, caught the steed a blow with his silken lash and seized its mane. In no time at all the stallion grew tame, bowed before him and said:

'Take me, Master. I shall obey you.'

Riding the black stallion home, the jigit showed it immediately to his sister – and the girl grew well again. When the hermit woman saw to her dismay that the boy had returned unharmed, she hurried off to tell the two sisters.

This time they said:

'Put another spell upon the girl so that she falls sick again, and tell the boy: "Your sister will get better only if you bring her the milky lake on which swims the golden duck with her ducklings." He will go to the milky lake and never return.'

Back home went the hermit woman and did as she was told: she put another spell on the girl and instructed the jigit to fetch the milky lake on which swam the golden duck with her ducklings. Once more the brother was in despair; where was he to find the milky lake and how would he carry a whole lake? This time the black stallion came to his aid.

'Jump up on my back,' it said, 'and I shall take you there.'

As they reached the lake, the stallion told its master:

'Whistle three times – and the lake with the golden duck and her ducklings will be wherever you wish it. But mind you whistle loudly – or we shall both be slain.'

Taking a great gulp of air into his lungs, the jigit let out three piercing

[111]

whistles that blew the tops off the trees. On the third whistle the milky lake rose up to the clouds, bearing the golden duck and ducklings with it, and disappeared from view.

When the jigit returned to his sister, he saw that the milky lake had formed before the hut, the golden duck with her ducklings was swimming upon it and his dear sister was walking along its banks completely cured.

'Thank you, dear Brother,' she said. 'Once more you have saved me from my malady.'

Of course the moment the two wicked sisters learnt of this they flew into a rage and told the hermit woman:

'This time you must not fail. Make the girl so lonely she will pine for a playmate – for Altynchech, the maid with the golden tresses who lives beyond the Mountains of Heaven. The boy will go there never to return; nobody has ever come back across the mountains alive.'

Again the hermit worked her spell, and the poor girl sat at the window pining for a playmate.

'Where am I to find a companion?' sighed the girl.

'On the other side of the Mountains of Heaven', said the hermit, 'stands a great palace in which dwells the lovely Altynchech. Ask your brother to bring her here.'

So the young girl beseeched her brother:

'Dear Brother, bring Altynchech here, I beg you.'

The jigit listened to his sister's request, saw her tears and rode off to seek the fair Altynchech beyond the Mountains of Heaven. After a hard journey he reached the palace and stood before its high walls.

'Shout three times', his stallion told him, 'as loudly as you can. At your cry, Altynchech will come out. Set her on my back behind you and I shall carry you both home. But, should your shout be too weak, we shall both be turned to stone!'

Taking a great gulp of air into his lungs, the jigit shouted thrice at the top of his voice. At the third call the stout walls crumbled and towards him came the fair Altynchech. In an instant he set her behind him and together they galloped home.

As soon as his sister set eyes on the maid, her sickness fell away as if it had never been. And Altynchech, too, laughed and played and was pleased to be with the brother and sister.

And so the days passed by in happy company.

One day, however, when the jigit was in the forest, he came upon a hunting party led by the padishah himself.

'Who are you and where do you live?' the padishah asked him.

'I am a simple hunter,' the other replied, 'and I live with my sister in the hut of an old hermit woman.'

'Do you shoot well and keep a well-stocked larder?' asked the padishah.

'That I do!' answered the jigit. 'I shoot as well as any man.'

The padishah was pleased with the lad's boldness and suggested they test their skill. First the padishah took aim and loosed an arrow at a flock of wild geese flying overhead – but his arrow flew wide into the trees.

The jigit laughed.

'Watch this,' he cried.

And he stretched his bow, let fly an arrow straight and true and brought down a goose from out of the sky. With a gracious bow he presented it to the padishah and bade him farewell. On returning to his palace, the padishah showed the goose to the two sisters.

'I was out hunting,' he explained, 'when I met a young hunter – what a marksman! I've never seen such shooting in my life!'

The sisters soon guessed whom the padishah had met. Afraid they would be found out, they hurried to the old hermit woman and ordered her to get rid of the jigit and his sister. Although the hermit seemed to agree, she was now sorry for the young pair; so she disobeyed the cruel order.

Meanwhile the jigit had fallen in love with the fair Altynchech and asked her to be his wife.

'I would gladly consent,' Altynchech said, 'but first you must rid your mother of her shame and get revenge on those who have wronged her.'

The jigit was astonished.

'Do we really have a mother?' he asked.

Altynchech then told the brother and sister the whole sad tale of their mother's fate. With hurt and anger in their hearts, they wanted to go at once to their poor mother, but Altynchech told them:

'First bake some pies and take them to your mother.'

As soon as the pies were ready, the brother and sister set off for the wayside hut where Altynchech had told them they would find their mother.

Now it so happened that, at about the time they were approaching the hut, the padishah chanced to glance through the window of his palace and saw the two figures carrying gifts to the hut of his former wife.

'Have those two brought here!' he told his guards. 'They should spit upon her, not take her gifts!'

When the pair were brought before him, he recognized the very archer he had encountered in the forest. And he soon learnt all that the brother and sister had heard from Altynchech.

In great remorse the padishah began to weep and tear out his hair; he now realized he had been tricked all these years by the two wicked sisters. Rushing to his wife, he fell to his knees before her and tearfully begged forgiveness for all he had done to her. And his wife was merciful:

'You were deceived by my sisters. Now you know I am quite blameless. We have found our dear children – Allah be praised. Let us then forget the past.'

The padishah embraced his dear wife and took her back to the palace. As for the two evil sisters, they were brought trembling and protesting before the padishah.

His judgment was severe but just: the wicked pair were tied to the tails of wild horses that were set galloping across the plains.

Afterwards the padishah married his son to the fair Altynchech and a grand wedding feast was held to which the whole of Tartary came. Such were the celebrations that they are still talked of to this day in the quiet of the Tartar evening.

Two Badgers

THERE was once a badger and his wife who lived off dormice and other rodents of the fields. One day, as they were in the meadow, an immensely large camel appeared on the horizon.

Said the badger to his wife:

'Come on, let's leave the mice and catch that camel.'

But his wife shook her head.

'We are both weary chasing after mice; the mice are weary too. Why bother to run after a camel that isn't tired? Should we really give up our mice for a camel?'

'Just think,' the badger persisted, 'that camel will stock our larder for many, many months. We need not hunt mice for ages and ages.'

Without more ado, he ran off in pursuit of the camel.

His wife remained. She caught a few tired mice, ate them and lay down to rest. Much, much later her husband returned with nothing to show for his hunting.

'Did you catch that camel?' asked his wife.

The badger could hardly speak from exhaustion.

'No, he escaped.'

'Did I not tell you – keep to hunting mice! Be mindful of the wise men's words: "Today's egg is better than tomorrow's chicken ..."'

The Clever Brothers

A POOR man told his three sons:

'My children, we have no riches, no cattle, no land of our own. You must therefore seek fortune of another kind: learn to understand everything. Let nothing escape your notice. In place of many cattle, you will possess keen minds; instead of land, you will have quick wits. With such riches you will fare no worse than any other.'

The brothers heard this many times and always took their father's advice. Thus, when he died, they came together, discussed their destiny and decided to go out into the world to seek their fortunes.

After many days upon the dusty road, they at last saw trees, then minarets and houses: a great city lay before them.

As they neared that city, the eldest brother stopped, stared intently at the ground and said:

'Brothers, a big camel passed this way but a short time ago.'

They walked on a short distance, then the second brother halted and, glancing to both sides of the road, he said:

'That camel was blind in one eye.'

They walked on farther, and the youngest brother observed:

'A woman and child were riding on that camel.'

After a time the three brothers were overtaken by a man on horseback. The eldest looked up and asked politely:

'You have lost something, have you not, my friend?'

'Yes, I have,' called the rider, pulling up.

'Is it not a camel you are seeking?' queried the eldest brother.

'You are right.'

'A big camel?'

'Yes.'

'Blind in one eye?' put in the second brother.

'Yes.'

'And would not a woman and child be riding upon it?' asked the youngest brother.

The horseman stared at the brothers.

'So, brigands, it is you who have stolen my camel!' he shouted. 'Speak up and tell me where you have hidden it.'

'We have never set eyes on your camel,' protested the brothers.

'Then how do you know so much about it?'

'Because we use our eyes and brains,' they replied. 'Make haste and ride to the east and you will find your camel.'

But the man would not listen. He had the three brothers dragged before the padishah, ruler of that land, and cast into the dungeons. Then he complained to the padishah.

'I was driving my herds to the hills; my wife and son were following on a big camel, blind in one eye. Somehow they lost their way and, as I was searching for them, I overtook three ruffians travelling on foot. I am sure they have stolen my camel; and I greatly fear they have killed my wife and son.'

'By what evidence do you make these charges?' asked the padishah.

'Before I could say a word,' explained the man, 'these three men told me my camel was big and blind in one eye, and was carrying a woman and child.'

The padishah thought for a moment.

'If, as you say, you told them nothing, and yet they were able to describe your camel so well, they must indeed have stolen it. Guards, have those men brought before me.'

The guards left the chamber and presently returned with the three brothers.

'Answer me, thieves,' cried the padishah, 'what have you done with this man's camel?'

'We are not thieves, nor have we seen his camel,' replied the brothers.

'Yet you described his camel to him,' broke in the padishah, 'without his telling you about it. How can you deny you stole it?'

'There is no mystery to that, O Padishah,' replied the eldest brother. 'Our father taught us to let nothing escape our notice; and we have spent much time learning to observe. That is how we could describe the camel without seeing it.'

The padishah laughed.

'Is it really possible to know so much about something you have never seen?' he asked disbelievingly.

'Certainly.'

'Then we must discover whether you are telling the truth.'

The padishah beckoned to his vizier and whispered in his ear. At once the vizier left the palace and returned several minutes later with two servants bearing a large chest.

Putting the chest down before the padishah, the servants moved aside. Meanwhile the three brothers watched closely, took note of the direction from which the chest had come, the manner in which it had been carried and the way it was set down upon the floor.

'Now then, rogues,' said the padishah, 'tell me what is in that chest ... if you can!'

'We have already told you we are not rogues, O Padishah,' protested the eldest brother. 'But, if you wish, I can tell you what is in the chest... That chest contains a small round object.'

'A pomegranate,' put in the second brother.

'That is not yet ripe,' added the third.

Thereupon the padishah ordered that the chest be opened. How astonished he was to find a green pomegranate inside! Taking it out, he held it up for all to see. Then, turning to the owner of the lost camel, he said:

'These men have proved they are not thieves. Indeed they are very clever. Seek your camel elsewhere, in the place where they told you to look, and bother me no more!'

[118]

The padishah called for food and drink to refresh and reward the three wise brothers.

'You are free to go where you will,' he told them. 'But first you must tell me all you observed in the order that it happened. First, how did you know that the man had lost a camel and what the camel was like?'

The eldest brother replied:

'The large tracks left in the dust told me that a very big camel had passed by. And, when I saw that the man who rode past us on the road kept glancing to all sides, I knew at once what he was seeking.'

'Good,' exclaimed the padishah. 'Now, which of you observed that the camel was blind in one eye?'

'It was I,' said the second brother. 'I noticed that the grass had been nibbled low on one side of the road, but untouched on the other.'

'Excellent,' said the padishah. 'And which of you guessed that a woman and child were riding the camel?'

'That was I,' answered the youngest brother. 'I noticed a spot where the camel had stopped and knelt down; there I saw the mark of a woman's boots on the sand close by. Second, smaller tracks told me the woman had a child with her.'

'That is truly remarkable,' said the padishah. 'But how did you know my chest contained an unripe pomegranate?'

Said the eldest brother:

'It was evident from the way your servants carried the chest that it was not at all heavy. As they were putting it down, I heard a clattering inside – as of some round object, not very large, rolling from one end to the other.'

Then the second brother spoke:

'And I surmised that, since the chest had been brought in from the garden and contained something small and round, that object had to be a pomegranate. For there are many pomegranate-trees growing beside your palace.'

'That is well said,' agreed the padishah; and he turned to the youngest brother.

'But how could you tell that the pomegranate was not yet ripe?'

'Now is the time of year', replied the young man, 'when all pomegranates are still green. You can see for yourself.'

And he pointed to the open window...

The padishah looked out and saw that the pomegranate-trees in his garden were, indeed, covered in green fruit. He could not but admire the brothers' unusual powers of observation and their quick wits.

'You may not be rich in worldly goods,' he said, 'but you are truly rich in wisdom.'

The padishah made the three clever brothers his palace counsellors. And they had none but their old father to thank for their good fortune.

 ## Who is the Mightiest in the World?

THERE once lived an old man and his wife with their only daughter. When the girl reached marrying age, her father thought to choose a husband for her.

'She shall wed whoever is the mightiest in the world,' he said.

So next day he set off across the plain to seek just such a husband. Somewhere along the way he came upon a patch of ice which was, as all ice is, very slippery. And it swept the old man off his feet. When he was on firm ground again, the old man stared admiringly at the ice.

'O mighty Ice!' he exclaimed, 'you truly are very strong to sweep my feet from under me. Pray be the husband of my only daughter.'

'Were I truly strong,' replied the ice, 'I should not melt in the rays of the sun.'

The old man scratched his head: the ice was right. So off he went to seek the sun. Finding him at last, he cried:

'O Sun, you who can melt the ice, surely you are stronger than him. Be the husband of my daughter.'

The sun sighed:

'Were I truly strong, the storm cloud would not shut out my rays.'

[122]

'Nodding his head slowly, the old man moved off to seek the storm cloud.

'Storm Cloud, Storm Cloud,' he called, 'you who can shut out the sun. Be the husband of my only daughter.'

But the storm cloud called down:

'Were I truly strong, I should not fall to earth as rain.'

On trudged the old man until he found the rain.

'O Rain,' he cried, 'you are certainly strong. Pray take my daughter for your wife.'

And the rain replied:

'Were I truly strong, the earth would not soak up my every raindrop.'

At that, the old man sank to his knees and appealed to the earth,

'O Earth, you are surely the mightiest in the world. You who can drink up every raindrop. Be, then, the husband of my daughter.'

But the earth replied:

'Were I truly mighty, the grass would not burst through my crown.'

Turning to the green grass, the old man cried:

'Grass, O Grass, you who can burst through the earth's crown; you must therefore be very strong. Be the husband of my only daughter.'

Said the grass:

'Man is mightier than I am. He cuts me down to my roots with his sharp scythe.'

Thereupon the old peasant went to man and said:

'O Man, you are indeed the mightiest in the world; you shall be the husband of my daughter. She is wise, hard-working and beautiful. She can even outride any horseman. Only you are worthy of her.'

The old man had come to the end of his journey. He had finally learnt that there is none mightier than man.

And so his daughter was wed to a young and handsome jigit.

The Poor Man and his Thousand Tanga

I WANT to tell you now the story of a poor man who worked very hard yet remained just as lowly as the day he was born. And so it was that, thinking to improve his lot, he set off to seek better fortune in the city.

He arrived at the gates of the great city of Tashkent and soon had rapped his knuckles on so many doors that the skin was torn and bleeding. But there are always some jobs to do in the city, and finally he found employment in some stables.

Such a good workman was he that his reputation spread and he was rarely idle: he chopped wood here, washed floors there, scrubbed wells, swept mosques clean, washed dusty feet. Never would he refuse a job no matter how hard and dirty it was.

As for the money he earned from his labours, he spent meagrely, only enough to keep body and soul together; all that remained he put into a small sack, telling himself:

'I shall toil on, save enough money and then return to my aul.'

In this way he worked unsparingly for five years and was able to set aside as much as a thousand tanga. Since that was a princely sum uncommon to the pocket of a humble man, he began to fret:

'What if I lose my fortune? If I carry it with me, I may be robbed or killed; if I hide it somewhere, it may be discovered and stolen – after all, the world contains many sly and wicked people. All my work will have been in vain.'

At last he made up his mind: he would entrust his thousand tanga to the safekeeping of the kashi – keeper of the city treasury.

'The townsfolk say he is a pious man,' he told himself. 'My money will be safe with him: I'll take it back when I am ready to return home.'

[125]

So the poor man went to the kashi.

'O most honourable Kashi,' he began, 'I want you to keep my money safe for me.'

The kashi took his small sack and said gravely:

'You do me a great honour, my friend. Rest assured, your fortune will be safe with me.'

As the poor man was leaving, the kashi counted out the money and put it in a large chest with innumerable other valuables.

Some months passed before the poor man was ready to leave for home. When he was ready, he went back to the kashi for his thousand tanga.

'O most honourable Kashi,' he said. 'May Allah bless you for guarding a poor man's fortune. I have now come to take back my money, for tomorrow I am leaving.'

The kashi glared at him.

'What are you talking about, ruffian?' he cried.

'Why, the thousand tanga I handed to you in a small sack to keep safe for me,' stuttered the poor man, becoming alarmed.

'Have you taken leave of your senses?' the kashi shouted. 'A thousand tanga, you say. Why, seven generations of your ancestors never laid eyes on a thousand tanga. So how could a ragged beggar like you earn a thousand? Be off before I set my dogs on you!'

The poor man begged the kashi to recall how he had brought the money to him; he described the exact day and time. But the kashi would not listen. He stamped his feet, waved his arms and screamed for his servants.

'Throw this beggar out of my house,' he roared. 'Beat him, kick him, set the dogs on him, the swindler!'

The kashi's servants fell upon the poor man, thrashed him most severely and flung him out of the house. He was chased all the way down the street by the kashi's dogs.

The poor man cursed his luck and wept tears of despair.

'All my hard work come to nothing!' he lamented. 'My money is lost! That greedy kashi has taken it all, every tanga.'

Just at that moment a woman was passing and, hearing the poor man's curses and seeing his tears, she said to him:

'Shame on you, Brother. Why do you, a grown man in a beard and turban, weep like a baby and curse like a bazaar vendor?'

'O my Sister,' said the poor man, 'if only you knew how I have been tricked! For five years I have laboured beyond my strength, eaten and slept little and, with the greatest hardship, saved a thousand tanga. Now it is all gone.'

And he told the story of how the kashi had tricked him.

'That is indeed a sorry tale,' she said. 'But do not despair. All is not yet lost. Come home with me and together we shall think of something.'

Once home she took a large box from her storeroom and gave instructions to her son:

'I am going to the kashi with this poor man. I want you to follow and, when I am in the kashi's house and he reaches out to take this box, run in quickly and say, "Father has returned with his goods and camels".'

'Very well, Mother,' answered the boy.

Thereupon the woman placed the box upon her head and set off with the poor man for the kashi's house. The woman's son followed at a distance. Outside the kashi's house, the woman told the poor man to wait awhile, then follow later.

As she entered the house, the kashi stared greedily at the large box on her head.

'What is your business with me, most gracious lady?' he inquired.

'No doubt you have heard of me?' she said. 'I am the wife of Rakhim, the rich merchant. My husband has gone with his camels to distant lands and left no news of his return. For many nights I have been unable to sleep for fear lest thieves break into my house and steal my fortune. This box contains all my money, much gold and precious stones. I beg you to keep it safe until my husband returns.'

Eagerly the kashi looked at the box and realized that it indeed contained many riches. He assured her that the fortune would be safer in his keeping than in the palace vaults, that every piece would be returned exactly as it was.

But the woman took back her box, seeming nervous.

'Are you quite sure it will be safe with you?' she asked.

'Of course, of course,' the kashi said impatiently. 'Everyone knows I am the most honest man in the city.'

At that very moment the poor man made his entry. And, as soon as the kashi set eyes on him, he pretended to be overjoyed.

'Here is your proof,' he said to the woman. 'Fate has sent this man here. I'll give him back his thousand tanga at once; he entrusted all his savings to me and this morning came to take them back. To my shame, I did not recognize him; I mistook him for a beggar and refused him the money. Now I remember well.'

With that the kashi reached into his chest, counted out a thousand tanga and presented that sum to the poor man with great ceremony.

'Well, gracious lady,' he said, 'you have now seen for yourself how safe other people's money is with me. Leave your box here and go in peace.'

He reached out for the box.

That was the signal for which the woman's son had been waiting. Running into the chamber, he shouted:

'Mother, Mother, come quickly. Father has returned with his goods and camels and is waiting for you.'

'There! Since my husband is back, I need not trouble you after all,' she said with a laugh. 'He will be able to guard his treasure without your help.'

With these words she took her box, set it back upon her head and left the kashi's house together with the poor man.

'So you see, Brother,' she said, 'never give way to despair. Allah, who sees all and raised the world without pillars, helps those who help themselves. Now, go back to your aul and live in peace and comfort. You have worked in this city long enough; it is time to spend your hard-earned money and enjoy it.'

Thus the poor man departed for home with his thousand tanga.

The Leaning Silver Birch

THERE once lived a man who was poor but as sharp as a bone needle. And in the same aul lived a rich man who thought himself smarter than the night is black.

The rich man was walking along one time when he spotted his neighbour in the distance leaning against a tree.

Coming up to him, he said:

'I have heard you possess the tongue of a magpie and the brain of a fox. But you cannot outwit me!'

'I could do so for sure,' replied the other. 'But not right now: I've left my box of tricks at home.'

The rich man gave a mocking laugh.

'Then run home and fetch it. I'll wait for you...'

'I would gladly do so,' replied the other. 'But you see, if I move away from this leaning silver birch, it will fall over.'

The rich man grinned.

'Enough of your excuses! Just go and get your box of tricks. I'll hold up the tree till you get back.'

And off went the quick-witted one, smiling to himself.

In the meantime the boaster waited and waited, holding up the tree. It was only when the villagers gathered to laugh at him that he realized he had been tricked. And never again did he boast about his quick wits.

Upon Jewel Mountain

In a certain aul in a time gone by, long before the reign of the Great Khan, there lived a widow with her only son Mirali. The widow combed goats' wool and took in washing to earn enough to feed them both. But, in the passing of the days, Mirali's mother told him:

'I have no strength to toil more, my son. You must make your own way and earn your keep.'

Thus Mirali took leave of his mother and went off to seek a living. He wandered from one place to the next, but nowhere could he find a master to give him work. At last he came to the house of a rich merchant.

'Do you need a workman, Bai?' he asked.

To his surprise, the merchant hired him straightaway and gave him quarters in which to rest. One day passed and then the next – yet still the merchant gave him no task. A third day went by and his new master seemed to have forgotten him.

Mirali began to wonder why the merchant had taken him on at all; so he went and asked:

'Shall I be getting any work, Master?'

'Of course, of course,' said the merchant gruffly. 'You shall work for me tomorrow; we are going on a long journey.'

On the morrow the rich merchant gave Mirali his orders: he was to slaughter and skin a big ox, fetch four large sacks and prepare two camels for the journey. The ox's hide and the sacks were loaded onto one of the camels, while the merchant climbed upon the other and Mirali walked alongside.

After a tiring journey, they finally arrived at the foot of a cold and misty mountain. The merchant halted his camels and instructed Mirali to take down the sacks and the ox's hide.

'Turn the ox's hide inside out,' commanded the merchant, 'and lie down upon it.'

Though he thought the order strange, Mirali did as he was told, not daring to disobey his rich master.

While Mirali was lying upon the hide, the merchant quickly rolled it into a bundle with the lad firmly trapped inside; the bundle was strapped and bound so that the boy could not escape. Whereupon the merchant hid behind a rock to wait...

Presently two great eagles swept down, attracted by the smell of meat on the ox's hide, seized the bundle in their claws and carried it off to the top of the mountain.

There they pecked and clawed at the bundle, soon tearing a hole in its side. When the hole was big enough, Mirali crawled out – much to the alarm of the giant birds who flew off in fright. Scrambling to his feet, Mirali looked desperately about him over the mountainside.

'Don't stand gawking, lad,' shouted the merchant from below. 'Throw down the precious stones that lie at your feet.'

Mirali looked down – the merchant was right! The ground was littered with jewels of every colour and shape – diamonds and rubies, sapphires and emeralds, turquoise and lapis lazuli, all sparkling in the cold rays of the sun.

The boy began to gather up the stones and throw them down to the merchant, who picked them up as fast as they fell and put them into his sacks.

Yet, as Mirali worked, a frightening thought came to him: how would he get down from the mountain?

To this question the merchant called back:

'Throw down more gems and I'll tell you.'

Trusting his master, the boy continued to toss down the gems. And, when the four sacks were full, the merchant hoisted them upon the backs of his camels and shouted up to Mirali:

'Well now, my lad, you know the sort of task I set my workmen. Look about you and you will see how I repay them – their bones are strewn all over the mountainside!'

With an evil chuckle the merchant rode off with his two laden camels.

Mirali was left alone upon Jewel Mountain. However hard he sought a way down, he saw nothing but abysses and precipices on every side – and human bones pecked clean by the birds and bleached by the sun. These were the skeletons of those who, like Mirali, had worked for the rich and villainous merchant.

The young lad saw no escape.

But just then, with a gust of wind that almost swept him off his feet, a huge eagle soared past his head. In a flash Mirali seized the eagle's legs and held on tightly; the eagle let out a screech, struggled up into the sky and wheeled round and round trying to shake off its unwanted passenger.

Finally it dropped slowly to the valley below, and thus Mirali saved himself from certain death.

Thanking Allah for his good fortune, he made the long journey back to town to search once more for work. Yet, to his dismay, who should approach him in the market-place but the old merchant. It was too late to hide.

It did not enter the merchant's head, however, that his former workman could still be alive. Taking the ragged boy for yet another humble soul eager for a job, he hired him and led him home.

In no time at all the merchant ordered Mirali to slaughter and skin an ox, prepare two camels and four sacks. And together they set off for the foot of that same cold and misty mountain. Just as before, the merchant instructed Mirali to lie upon the ox's hide and wrap himself up in it.

But the lad was wiser now. Pretending to be slow and dim-witted, he said to the merchant:

'Master, I am clumsy and stupid; please show me how it should be done.'

'What is there to understand, fool!' shouted the merchant. 'Just watch me closely.'

With that the merchant stretched himself upon the hide ... In an instant Mirali had rolled up the hide with the merchant inside it, strapped it tight and stepped back behind a rock.

Although the merchant kicked and struggled, he could do nothing to free himself. And, when his strength gave out, two great eagles swooped down, clasped the ox's hide and bore it aloft to the mountain top. Once there, they began to tear at it with their beaks and claws. On seeing the merchant, however, they flew off in alarm. The merchant jumped to his feet and screamed down the mountain at his stupid workman.

'Come, Bai, do not waste time,' called Mirali with a laugh. 'Throw down the gems, as I did for you.'

Only then did the merchant recognize his former workman; he shook with rage and not a little fear.

'How did you escape from the mountain?' he cried.

'Throw down the jewels and, when I have filled the four sacks, I shall tell you,' replied Mirali.

The merchant tossed down gems as fast as his arms would work; and the lad picked them up as quickly as they fell. When the sacks were full, he placed them upon the backs of the camels and called:

'So you wish to know how to escape? Come, Bai, look about you. The bones of your former workmen whom you left to die are all around you. Ask them how to get down from the mountain!'

And, turning the camels round, Mirali set off for town, leaving the merchant behind on the mountaintop.

The merchant rushed about on the mountain, hurling threats and screaming pleas.

All in vain.

For there was none to hear his cries but the skeletons of his dead workmen.

Obdurman the Clever Huntsman

As Obdurman the huntsman walked through the forest to inspect his bird traps, he was pestered by a magpie that kept flapping about his head and cawing most annoyingly. Obdurman finally lost patience and seized the bird by its tail. Thrusting it into his pouch, he said:

'Now sit tight and hold your peace – or you'll end up in a stew.'

As he went on his way, he spotted three blue eggs in a rock cleft, and he decided to take one home for his children.

After some time he arrived at the glade in which he had set his traps. But to his dismay the traps were torn and the game was gone. Noticing large tracks leading into the depths of the forest, Obdurman hurried off in pursuit of the culprit.

'Right, thief,' he mumbled, 'I'll teach you a lesson; you won't come round my traps again!'

In his rage he forgot to mark his way and presently found himself quite lost in the dark forest. He was cursing his foolishness when, to his relief, he caught sight of a cottage through the trees.

'That must be where the thief lives,' he thought, growing very cross again. And he rushed into the cottage without so much as a knock. And then stopped short!

For there towering above him was a giant, fierce and huge, plucking grouse and scowling at the intruder. Obdurman knew it was useless to run away, for the giant would certainly catch him and break all his bones.

Hiding his fear, Obdurman shouted:

'Hey, you seventh son of a donkey! What's the idea stealing my grouse?'

[136]

The giant's eyes widened at such boldness from a fellow no taller than his kneecap. Taken aback, he muttered:

'Well, sir, if the grouse is yours, let's share it.'

'Certainly not!' cried Obdurman. 'Why should I share what is rightfully mine? I set the traps. The whole grouse belongs to me. If you don't give it back this instant, I'll have to teach you a lesson!'

'You speak boldly for one so small,' said the giant. 'I could squeeze you to pulp if I wished. I'll tell you what: let's test our strength. The victor will have the grouse.'

The giant picked up a stone and continued,

'You see this stone? If you can squeeze juice from it, I'll take your word that you are as strong as you are bold.'

'First you squeeze juice from it,' answered Obdurman, 'then I'll show you what I can do.'

The giant took the stone in his huge fist and ground the stone into fine sand. Opening his fist, he cried in triumph:

'D'you see that!'

'See what?' said Obdurman with a sneer. 'You said squeeze juice from the stone. And all you've got is sand. Just watch this.'

Taking the egg from his pocket, Obdurman crushed it in his hand until the yolk trickled between his fingers. When the giant saw that, he was astonished and really did suspect that the huntsman was stronger than himself. But he was not ready to give in.

'Let's see which of us is faster,' he cried. 'Which can catch a bird in full flight.'

'All right,' replied Obdurman calmly, 'but you show me first what you can do. Then I'll better it.'

They left the cottage and went into a large clearing in the forest. As the giant caught sight of a flock of birds, he raced after them, leapt upwards and ... fell to the ground with a great crash!

Obdurman roared with laughter.

'The only birds you can catch are in other people's traps,' he said. 'Now watch me. Do you see that speck up there in the sky?'

[137]

As the giant strained his eyes to follow the direction of Obdurman's gaze, the wily huntsman quickly took the magpie from his pouch, ran a few paces and held the bird aloft, crying in triumph:

'Got it! Got it!'

When the giant saw the magpie fluttering helplessly in Obdurman's hand, he was astonished.

'Can this huntsman really be stronger and swifter than me?' he wondered to himself. 'I'll set him one last task – and that will settle it.'

'Let's see which of us can whistle the loudest,' he said.

'As you wish,' replied Obdurman.

The giant let out such a whistle that it blew Obdurman off his feet. When he had recovered, he said to the giant:

'Now it's my turn. But you had better cover your eyes and ears or you'll be blind and deaf for the rest of your days!'

The old giant bound his eyes and ears tightly with a cloth, lest he should really go blind and deaf. Then Obdurman snatched up a stout stick and hit him over the head as hard as he could.

'Well, Giant, did I whistle loudly enough?' he said. 'If you like, I can shout as well, only it will knock all your teeth out.'

Unbinding the cloth, the giant said hastily:

'No, No! Don't shout. Goodness, gracious me! As it is, I can still see stars from your whistling.' And he thought to himself: 'It's no use trying to outwit this fellow; I'll have to think of some way to get rid of him.'

'Well now, huntsman,' the giant growled, 'since the hour is late you'll have to spend the night with me.'

After he had given the huntsman food and drink, the giant asked:

'What can you do when you're asleep?'

Obdurman guessed that the giant had something up his sleeve, so he replied boldly:

'The moment I'm asleep I turn into a tree-stump. And you?'

The giant had to admit he could not turn himself into anything.

'But, as soon as I'm asleep, fire pours from my nostrils and smoke from my mouth.'

After thus talking for a time, the two men lay down on the floor of the cottage. It was not long before the giant was snoring loudly. Fire poured from his nostrils, smoke belched from his mouth. That was Obdurman's chance. He tiptoed quietly from the cottage and brought back a rotten tree-stump. This he covered with his cloak and then concealed himself behind the stove.

By and by, the giant's snoring stopped, the fire and smoke subsided and he opened his eyes. He stood up and snarled:

'Now I'll get my revenge on this insolent fellow!'

Seizing a huge boulder, he dashed it down on the cloak-covered tree-stump, scattering sawdust in all directions and making himself splutter and sneeze.

'What a bag of old rubbish he is!' roared the giant. 'He's stuffed full of sawdust.'

The giant lay down once more, and soon fire and smoke were pouring from him. In the morning he awoke and could hardly believe his eyes: there lay Obdurman beside the great boulder – as large as life.

'Hey, Giant,' said Obdurman drowsily, 'what's the idea, throwing sand on me in the night?'

The giant's eyes grew wide in amazement; he did not know what to say.

'I give in,' he conceded at last. 'Take all my gold, as much as you can carry, but go home and leave me in peace! I'll never touch your traps again.'

'Hmmmmm!' hemmed Obdurman, thinking it over. 'Let's see your gold.'

The giant dragged an enormous sack full of gold from the corner and offered it to the huntsman. The giant himself could barely drag it along – that's how heavy it was.

'To pay for your wrongdoing, you must carry this sack home for me,' said Obdurman craftily, knowing full well that he could not carry it himself.

The giant was too scared to argue with the huntsman, so he humped the sack of gold on his back and staggered out of the cottage with it. He stumbled and groaned, limped and moaned along the forest path; and all the while Obdurman ran alongside, urging him on:

'Faster, faster! It's as light as duck's feathers.'

At long last they reached Obdurman's humble cottage at the edge of the forest.

'Put the sack in my barn,' ordered Obdurman, 'while I let my wife know you're here. We must prepare something worthy of our guest.'

As he entered the cottage, he told his wife:

'A giant has come home with me, Wife, but don't show him you're scared. He's thoroughly stupid. We'll teach him a lesson he'll never forget. When I ask you what we have to eat, you must say: "All that's left is the head of one big giant and the flesh of the small giant we dined on yesterday." Say nothing more.'

Thereupon Obdurman led the giant into his home and shouted to his wife.

'Wife, bring food for our guest.'

'What shall I serve him?' asked the wife. 'All that's left is the head of one big giant and the flesh of the small giant we dined on yesterday. Will that do?'

On hearing these words, the giant quite lost his wits: he sprang up and rushed from the cottage without a backward glance. As he stumbled through the forest, he banged his head on firs and scratched his face on pines before finally, in his headlong rush, he tripped over a fox and came down with a crash.

'Why are you in such a hurry?' asked the fox. 'Why is your head so bruised and your face so scratched?'

'I am escaping from the terrible huntsman Obdurman,' replied the giant. 'He is a most fearsome giant-eater!'

And he recounted his story to the fox.

'What a stupid giant you are!' laughed the fox. 'In these parts he is the most foolish of all the humans. He has tricked you. And you were taken in. Let's go back together and you shall deal with him properly.'

The giant believed the fox and went with her to deal with Obdurman. But the huntsman spied them coming and, advancing to meet them, he called:

'Well done, Fox! That huge ruffian nearly escaped me. Bring him here quickly so that we can cut him up for dinner and I can give you your share.'

'Oi-yoi-yoi-yoi-yoi!' wailed the giant, stopping in his tracks. 'That fox is in league with the huntsman. The treacherous animal! I'll teach her a lesson.'

Grabbing the fox by the tail, the giant threw her to the ground so hard that the stuffing was knocked right out of her. Then he took to his heels once more and disappeared into the forest.

All the while he could hear Obdurman shouting after him:

'Hold him, catch him, don't let that rogue escape! I want him for dinner.'

And the wily Obdurman laughed till his sides shook. Then he skinned the fox, made his wife a warm fur hat and, from that time on, lived in peace and prosperity.

The Golden Vase

It is said that long ago, when the Siberian rivers, daughters of the mighty Lord Baikal, ran fast and free, there lived a Tartar khan named Sanad, lord of forty thousand tents.

That khan grew weary of dwelling in one place, so he resolved to lead his people on a long journey to new grazing lands, where the grass was tender and full-grown. But the way ahead would be hard; there would not be enough provisions for the whole clan.

So the khan gave out an order:

NOT ONE OLD MAN OR WOMAN
SHALL ACCOMPANY US ON OUR
JOURNEY

THEY MUST ALL BE KILLED

It was a most cruel command, and it lay heavy on people's hearts. But the khan's will was law – to sin against him was to sin against Allah himself.

There was one young man, Temuchin, however, who vowed he would not kill his father: he would conceal the old man in a canvas sack and take him to the new grazing grounds in secret – though he knew he risked death.

Sanad Khan led his subjects from their homeland and, with their flocks, they set out for the far-off lands to the north. With Temuchin went the old man, concealed in the canvas sack slung across a horse's back. Unbeknown to the others, the boy gave his father food and drink and, whenever they made camp and it grew dark, he would untie the sack and let his father out so that he might stretch his aching limbs.

[144]

This continued as the caravan wound its way across the land until, at last, they came to the shore of a great lake under a towering cliff. There Sanad Khan commanded them to halt and camp for the night.

As one of the khan's attendants went down to the water's edge, he saw a strange and wonderful sight: there in the transparent water lay something that sparkled and gleamed. Taking a closer look, he saw it

was a large golden vase. He hastened back to his master to report his find: a precious golden vase lay beneath the waves hard by the shore of the lake.

Sanad Khan immediately gave orders for his men to dive into the depths of the water to bring up the precious vase. But since no man among them could swim or dive – they had never lived by a sea or deep river – nobody came forward. In the end the khan commanded them to draw lots.

The first lot fell to a young attendant of the khan; he dived into the lake and vanished beneath the waves.

Again lots were cast. And this time it fell to another of the khan's attendants. He too dived into the water and was never seen again. In this manner many men lost their lives.

But the stubborn khan would not give in. One after another his men dived, unprotesting, into the lake. And drowned. For none dared emerge without the vase.

At last it came to the turn of Temuchin; before diving into the lake, he took leave of his father.

'Farewell, Father, we are both doomed to die.'

'Tell me, my son,' his father asked, 'why must we die?'

The boy explained that it had fallen to him to dive to the bottom of the lake for the golden vase.

'And no one has yet found the vase,' he said sadly. 'I am bound to drown. Then you will be discovered and put to death.'

The old man heard him out, then said sagely:

'Do you not understand? The vase is not at the bottom of the lake at all. What you see is its reflection. It stands on top of the steep cliff. Why did none of you young people think of that?'

And he told his son how to climb the cliff, take the vase and deliver it to the khan.

'It will not be hard to find: the vase sparkles so, you can see it from afar. But the cliff is steep and you must be careful. Wait until mountain goats appear, then find a way of startling them. When they rush up the

cliff, they will knock down the vase in their haste. Waste no time: catch
it quickly lest it fall into the lake and be lost forever.'

Temuchin thanked his father for this wisdom and set off.

It was not easy to climb the rugged cliff. He clutched at shrubs and
sharp rocks, scratching his face and hands until his skin was raw and
his clothes were in tatters. Finally, when he had almost reached the top,
he caught sight of the golden vase, standing high and proud on a lofty
pinnacle. But he knew he could not scale that rock.

So he heeded his father's advice and waited for mountain goats to
appear. Sure enough, he did not have long to wait, for several goats came
into sight on the cliffside. When the boy gave a loud shout, they
scampered to and fro, pushing one another until they knocked down
the golden vase. As it rolled down the mountainside, Temuchin swiftly
snatched it up and held it safely in his arms, then climbed down the
mountain.

'How did you fetch this vase from the bottom of the lake?' asked
Sanad Khan in amazement.

'It was not there I found it,' the boy replied, 'but on top of yonder
mountain. What we saw in the water was only its reflection.'

The khan wondered at the boy's wisdom but asked no more questions.
At once he gave the order for the caravan to move on towards the north.

At the end of the day they came to a great desert. The sun burnt down
so fiercely that all the grass was scorched and the ground baked hard.
No river, not even a narrow brook was to be seen. All the people and
sheep began to suffer a terrible thirst. And, although Sanad Khan dispatched horsemen in all directions to seek water, they found nothing
but parched, scorched land.

The people were in despair, certain they would die.

Unnoticed, Temuchin crept away to his father.

'What are we to do, Father?' he asked tearfully. 'We are all dying
of thirst; so too are the sheep.'

'Set free a young sheep,' said the old man, 'and watch it closely.
Wherever it stops and sniffs the ground, there you must dig for water.'

The boy ran back home and set loose a young sheep. It wandered off across the desert, its head close to the sand ... At last it came to a halt and began eagerly to sniff at the hot earth, breathing in great gulps of air.

'Dig here!' shouted Temuchin to the men who accompanied him.

The men started to dig and soon reached a cool underground spring. The entire clan drank its fill and was grateful to the young lad for saving every life. Yet the khan was suspicious.

'How did you find water in this dry land?' he asked.

'I followed certain signs,' answered the boy.

The khan was still very curious, but he had to move the caravan on. After several days and nights they again halted and pitched camp. And, during the night, rain poured down, flooding the camp and putting out their fires. Chilled and wet, the people tried to make up their fires again. But everything was too damp.

Then someone sighted a campfire on a distant hill.

Straightaway the khan gave orders for his men to fetch a light and bring it back to camp.

Men rushed to do his bidding. First one, then a second, then a third scrambled up the hill to the fire that burnt beneath the thick branches of a large spruce. They each took away a burning log – yet not one succeeded in carrying it as far as the camp. For the heavy rain extinguished the fire.

Sanad Khan grew very angry. Anyone who returned without a lighted log would be put to death.

'What is to be done, Father?' asked Temuchin. 'How is the fire to be carried from the hilltop to our camp?'

'Do not take the burning logs,' replied the old man. 'The rain will put them out before you get back. Take instead a large pot with you and fill it with smouldering embers. Only thus will you bring back fire to the camp.'

The boy did as his father said and brought down a potful of glowing embers from the hilltop. The people made up their fires, dried and warmed themselves and cooked their food.

[148]

When Sanad Khan learnt who had brought the fire, he called Temuchin to him once more.

'How did you learn about the embers?' shouted the khan. 'Where did
you gain such wisdom?'

This time the boy had to confess that it was his old father's counsel
that had saved them.

'Where is your father?' asked the khan.

'I brought him with us in a canvas sack,' admitted Temuchin, sure
he had now sealed the fate of both his father and himself.

But the khan grew thoughtful.

'Have the old man brought before me,' he ordered.

And when Temuchin's father was brought from his canvas sack, Sanad
Khan said:

'I was wrong to think the old are a burden on the young. Age has
wisdom. Old man, hide no longer. You may ride with us freely and be
our guide and counsellor.'

Zilyan

THERE once lived a man as poor and humble as a body has ever been. All the same, he brought up his children to be sharp, nimble and hardworking.

The first son could tell any object however far away by its smell alone.

The second son could fire an arrow so straight it would hit even the most distant target.

And the third was so strong he could lift any weight.

The daughter Gulnara was a most uncommon needlewoman, the best there was in the Tartar homelands.

So the old man was proud of his children and, when his time came, he died content. With their father gone, the four children managed the household themselves, the boys hunting and the girl cooking, keeping house and trading her exquisite needlework.

However, an evil genie resolved to steal that beautiful and clever girl and began to follow her wherever she went. But her brothers were ever watchful and tried not to let their dear sister out of sight.

Soon after their father's burial the three brothers went hunting, leaving Gulnara alone in the cottage. When they set off, they gave her strict warning not to open the door to anyone before their return. With that, they locked and bolted the door and rode away.

Since he was watching the girl's every movement, the evil genie knew immediately that nobody was home save the young girl. So he broke down the door and stole the girl away. Of course, when the brothers returned, they found the house empty.

Realizing it was the work of the genie, they set out in pursuit; they had many mountains to cross, many valleys to traverse and many rivers to ford. Yet they kept to the genie's tracks.

The first brother walked ahead, sniffing the air and following the genie's scent. With his nose in the air, he led the brothers through a forest until they came to a dark cavern, the lair of the evil genie. And there inside, sure enough, sat their poor sister, the genie snoring by her side.

Creeping into the dark cavern, the brothers snatched up their sister and carried her off without even waking the slumbering genie. And away they hastened on their long homeward journey.

At the end of the day, tired and footsore, they came to a lake where they had to take a rest; lying down by the lakeside, all four were soon in a deep sleep.

Meantime the genie had woken up to find Gulnara gone. In a fearful rage he rushed from his dark cavern and flew off like a whirlwind in search of the fugitives. In no time at all he had reached the lake and spotted the group sleeping. Swooping down like an eagle, he seized the girl and soared up with her into the clouds.

The girl's cries woke her brothers, but it was too late: the genie and their sister were no more than a tiny speck in the sky.

Quickly snatching up his trusty bow, the second brother let fly an arrow which sped to its mark and tore off the genie's right arm. He then loosed a second arrow – and this flew straight and true, piercing the genie's body and making him drop the girl.

She fell through the air like a stone and would surely have crashed to the ground had not the third brother dashed to her aid. Just in time he caught her in his strong arms before she hit the hard earth.

Thus they all returned home safe and happy.

Gulnara was so grateful to her brothers that she at once set to making a beautiful zilyan, thinking to herself:

'I'll give this zilyan to the brother who did most to save me.'

But, when she asked who had done most to rescue her, she received the following answers:

Said the eldest brother:

'Without me we should not have discovered your trail. For I was able to follow the genie's scent.'

The second brother added:

'Were it not for me, the genie would have carried you off again. I shot him with my arrows.'

And the third brother said:

'If I had not caught you in time, you would have crashed to the ground.'

Gulnara listened to each one and was silent. She thought and thought, yet she still did not know which brother most deserved the beautiful zilyan.

Nor does she to this day. Do you?

Proud Ilbatyr in the Land of Cathay

Whoever strays from the fold is meat for the bear.
Whoever falls behind is meat for the wolf.

So say the old hunters of the Irenduk Hills. Our tale is of a jigit from those hills who became separated from his people. But not of his own will.

In a lonely aul at the foot of a mountain lived an old hunter and his wife with their only son Ilbatyr. The son loved his native land more than all else. And when he came of age he would lead his companions on hunting trips deep into the forest and, when called to service, he would lead them into battle against their enemies.

It happened one time, as Ilbatyr was riding to a distant aul, that he had to spend the night in the forest. While he slept, a fierce wind sprang up making the forest roar, the cliffs and mountain caverns wail, and blotting out the sky with black clouds. And, as the storm clouds descended on the forest, they enveloped Ilbatyr and carried him high into the dark night.

In his heavy slumber Ilbatyr knew nothing of his journey. Thus, when he awoke, he could not comprehend how he had come to a new and strange land.

Hidden in the storm cloud had been a wizard, who had borne Ilbatyr far across the roof of the world into the land of Cathay.

For many years that wizard had followed Ilbatyr, watching him grow to manhood and become a valiant warrior. At last his moment had come to seize the jigit and take him off to join the wizard's army. Thus it was that many a young jigit had been spirited away, just like Ilbatyr, to guard the wizard's empire and fight against his foes. Proud Ilbatyr, though,

[154]

was the wizard's greatest prize: he was chosen to be commander of the wizard's army.

The wizard had three daughters in his palace. Summoning them to him, he bade them entertain the new warrior and distract him with their charms. When the maidens came before Ilbatyr, they admired his proud and handsome bearing; they led him to a grand hall, where there awaited him a rich array of delicacies such that made the mouth water just to look at them. They told him diverting stories, sang sweet songs and played beautiful music.

Yet the proud Ilbatyr neither ate, nor drank, nor listened. He stood tall and grave, as cold as a stone statue. Nothing the wizard's daughters did could melt his disdain.

When the wizard saw that his daughters' charms had failed, he grew angry.

[155]

'Why be so stubborn, jigit?' he asked. 'I've waited many years for this moment. I possess no sons, no worthy warrior to lead my soldiers into battle, nor any trusty friend to guard my treasure. Serve me well and I shall grant you whatever you desire. Take any of my daughters. You shall live more richly than any emperor.'

Ilbatyr heard him out then broke his stony silence.

'I crave for none of your wealth,' he said, 'nor any of your daughters. All I wish is to return to my native land. Our Tartar hills are higher than your palace, our meadows are softer than your thickest carpets, our forests are greener than your orchards, the water of our streams is sweeter even than sherbet.'

But the wizard persisted.

'Do you miss your kinsfolk? What is it you need? Tell me and I shall have it brought here this instant.'

'That which I have left behind cannot be replaced. Nothing can match our hills, our forests, our meadows, our streams. And I cannot live without them.'

The wizard promised to build a hill as tall as Ilbatyr's and that night summoned all his serfs to bring stones from far and near to raise a mountain beside the palace. When Ilbatyr awoke, he beheld the towering mountain thrusting its peak high into the clouds. Yet it was nothing but bare stone – no trees, no grass, no flowers, not even cheering birdsong. As he climbed the mountain, his thoughts were of his native hills and the many happy times he had hunted in the forests, bathed in the swift-flowing rivers.

The wizard did not give up. He tried to create everything as it was in Ilbatyr's homeland. At his command majestic trees grew on the mountain slopes, birds and beasts came to dwell in the wooded hills. But Ilbatyr was not to be consoled.

> *If only my arms were wings*
> *I would soar through the sky*
> *Home to my own dear kinsmen.*

[156]

Such was the lament he composed in his sad and lonely mood. Nothing could comfort him. Not even the wizard's lovely daughters. For they knew none of the songs sung in Ilbatyr's land.

Many a time Ilbatyr tried to escape; yet each time he was overtaken and brought back. Finally he was put in chains and thrown into a dungeon.

In his native aul there was great alarm when he did not return and nobody knew of his whereabouts. No one knew whether he had drowned in a sudden torrent, stumbled off a cliff or been devoured by wild beasts. Several times his kinsmen searched the forest for him, but no trace was found. His poor parents became sick with grief and it was not long before his mother died.

But news never came of the missing jigit.

Meanwhile, in the wizard's dungeon, Ilbatyr grew more and more feeble; as the weeks grew into months, his strength all but drained away and he could no longer stand. To keep him alive, the wizard had him brought up into the sunshine. And from then on he lay, waiting for death's release, beneath a pomegranate tree in the garden. His only friend was Tashbulat, another of the wizard's captives.

'Many a jigit has met his end here,' said Tashbulat. 'No true warrior will bow to this evil tyrant. But there may be a way of escape.'

And Tashbulat unfolded his plan.

'If you ask leave to go home to take a last look at your native aul, the wizard will, of course, refuse. But he might send one of us in your place. Then you can send a message, bidding jigits from your aul to come to your aid.'

Ilbatyr agreed to the plan.

'All right, I consent to serve you,' Ilbatyr told the wizard. 'But first I must know whether my folk are alive and my kinsmen still remember me. Take me to my aul for a day or, if not me, send a messenger on my behalf.'

The wizard was delighted that he had tamed the proud Ilbatyr at last. So he assented to dispatch a messenger of Ilbatyr's choosing.

Tashbulat came forward and the wizard pronounced a magic chant, enveloping the jigit in a dark cloud, which lifted him far over the hills and forests, over the Great Wall itself, before setting him down in Ilbatyr's aul. At once Tashbulat sought out Ilbatyr's father and told him all the news of his son. The old man was overjoyed to hear that his son was still alive and he immediately spread the glad news throughout the aul. When the jigits learned of their brother's appeal, they prepared their bows and arrows, sharpened their swords and assembled their finest horses – ready to do battle with the wizard.

For many days and nights the jigits rode towards the wizard's land and on the fortieth day they arrived at the Great Wall of Cathay, beyond which lay the wizard's palace. But no one could cross that mighty wall: day and night it belched smoke and flames and roared fiercely.

The jigits drew back from the wall to take counsel. How were they to reach the wizard's domain? The wall was so high and thick and the sky above was filled with black smoke. Sensing their despair, Tashbulat stood before them and cried:

'Listen, brothers of proud Ilbatyr! I remember the wizard's magic chant. Perhaps it will help us to cross the wall. Feed and water your steeds, sharpen your arrows and swords, rest well, then mount up and ride hard at the wall. As soon as you reach it, I'll say the chant and our horses will rise into the air. Only hold on tight. If you fall from your horse, you will surely die!'

Each rider did as Tashbulat said: they sharpened their arrows and swords, watered and fed their horses, then mounted them and rushed like the wind at the Great Wall. The instant they reached it, Tashbulat spoke the magic words. And at once the steeds reared up and rose into the air. They flew faster and faster, above the clouds, over the mountains, and landed outside the wizard's palace.

The wizard was away, but the palace guards advanced to seize them. Tashbulat addressed them:

'Throw down your arms, open the gates. Jigits from Ilbatyr's aul have come to set us free!'

[158]

Recognizing Tashbulat and stirred by his words, the guards threw open the gates and led the jigits to the wizard's dungeons. At once all the prisoners were set free. Meanwhile Ilbatyr lay beneath the pomegranate tree, his strength almost gone. Yet, the moment he sipped the water brought from his native streams, his old strength surged through him and he sprang to his feet, crying:

'Thank you, my brothers! Thank you for the water of life. I am now fit to depart with you for our homeland.'

Having freed all the captives, the band of men destroyed the dungeons and got ready in haste for their homeward journey. Tashbulat taught the magic words to each jigit, so that each could mount his horse, rise high into the air and fly above the wall, forests and open plains.

As soon as Ilbatyr stepped back upon his native soil, breathed in the refreshing air and drank the spring water from his native streams, his strength was even greater than before, his eyes glowed with happiness and the colour returned to his cheeks. Once again he led the jigits to hunt in the forests and hills. And, when the spring work was ended, they held a great festival, a Saban Tui, at which all the jigits tried their strength and skill in games and dancing.

And, of course, the whole aul rejoiced when Ilbatyr was hailed as the strongest and most skilful jigit in the Tartar tribes.

Glossary

aida	come on, let's go
Allah	name of God used by Moslems
ata	father, term of respect for an older man
aul	a settlement, group of tents
bai	a rich man
Bashkir	Tartar-speaking people of mixed origin who today inhabit the area south-east of Kazan
bish-barmak	literally 'five fingers' – a meat dish with noodles
Cathay	name given by Marco Polo to what is now part of China. Black Cathay (Karakitai), however, was a land in Central Asia
Chingis Khan	real name Temuchin, Tartar–Mongol leader (1162–1227) who welded all the Tartar–Mongol tribes into a single nation and whose empire extended from the Pacific Ocean to the Black Sea, including Central Asia, China, Russia and Iran
jigit	a 'brave', young man of courage and skill
jinn	a good or evil spirit
kashi	money-lender or city treasurer
khan	ruler of the nomad tribes
kumis	fermented mare's milk, an intoxicating and refreshing drink: 'It is pungent on the tongue like rape wine when drunk, and when a man has finished drinking, it leaves a taste of milk of almonds on the tongue, and it makes the inner man most joyful and also intoxicates weak heads, and greatly provokes urine.' (Marco Polo)
kurai	a long reed-pipe cut from the stem of a meadow plant
muezzin	man who serves in a mosque, calls the faithful to prayer
mullah	Mohammedan priest
padishah	a ruler or king

[161]

Glossary

saban-tui	a festival held in the spring (*saban* – a plough) with songs and storytelling, horse-racing, boxing and wrestling
shah	ruler or king
shaitan	the Devil
tanga	money; the Russian word for money (*dengi*) comes from the name *Chingis* Khan
vizier	adviser to the khan or shah
yurta	a tent made of a framework of wood covered in felt made from lambswool. The round bee-hive shape of the yurta is well suited to withstand the blazing sun and the icy winds of the plains
zilyan	sheepskin coat

Commentary on Tartar Folk Tales

> *If I were Lord of Tartary*
> *Myself, and me alone,*
> *My bed should be of ivory,*
> *Of beaten gold my throne*
> Walter de la Mare, 'Tartary'

If indeed you were Lord or Lady of Tartary, where would we seek your throne of beaten gold, the era of your ivory bed?

To find out, we must fly in our time machine to an empire standing like some great giant astride the two continents of Europe and Asia, far vaster than that of Ancient Rome – to an age over 800 years ago, when that first illustrious Tartar lord, Chingis Khan (sometimes known as Ghengis, or Jengis, Khan), was becoming the greatest conqueror and most feared man in the world.

Tartary, the heartland of our stories, may loosely be located in the valleys, plains and foothills of Central Asia. It lies between the kilometre-and-a-half deep, transparent Lake Baikal to the east and the world's largest inland sea, the Caspian, to the west. Its northern border stretches beyond the grassy and wooded steppe of central Russia into the forests of fir and pine that descend to the frozen Arctic Ocean. And in the south its natural backdrop are the Mountains of Heaven, thrusting their snow-capped peaks six and a half kilometres into the clouds. The Himalayas and Pamirs are situated in the centre of Tartary, flanked by the Tien Shan and Altai to the east, the Hindu Kush and Elbrus to the west.

The land within these boundaries is traversed by two great rivers, the Jaxartes, or Syr Darya, and the Oxus, or Amu Darya, both rising in the melting snow of the mountains to the south and wending their way slowly and finally into the Aral Sea.

[163]

Commentary on Tartar Folk Tales

It was along the valleys of these two great rivers and among the foothills of the world's largest mountain range that the culture and commerce of Central Asia took root and blossomed. It was here too that the caravans from China to Europe marketed their wares. And to this Mecca came the faithful, making the golden journey to Samarkand. For, when all is said and done,

> *Death has no repose*
> *Warmer and deeper than that Orient sand*
> *Which hides the beauty and bright faith of those*
> *Who made the Golden Journey to Samarkand.*
> James Elroy Flecker, 'The Golden Journey to Samarkand'

Because of the geographical variations, the people of this land led different lives. There were the settled dwellers in the oases and cities – of Samarkand, Tashkent, Bokhara and Khiva (the setting for several of our tales: 'The Clever Brothers', 'The Poor Man and his Thousand Tanga', 'Yerensay'). There were the inhabitants of the northern forests busy with their hunting, trapping, fishing and beekeeping and living in small semi-nomadic settlements (see 'Abzelil', 'Shuralee', 'Obdurman', 'The Bear and the Bees'). And finally there were the pastoral nomads of the plain, who raised horses, sheep, goats, camels and a few cattle (see 'Aldar-Kose', 'The Fern Girl', 'Saran and Yumart', 'The Golden Vase'). These last nomadic tribes were constantly on the move, pitching their bee-hive-shaped felt tents, or yurtas, to the north in summer, where the grass was lush for grazing, and to the south in winter to avoid the heavy northern snowfalls. Since security was vital, for there could be no walls to defend them, they had to be ever vigilant and ready to move on should danger threaten.

Who exactly are the Tartars?

That is not an easy question to answer, for the early nomads of Central Asia kept few records, partly owing to their enforced mobility. Historically we know of various nomadic civilizations through their scattered cultural 'droppings' of oral records and artefacts. And now and again a bold, inquisitive explorer from the West would arrive to chronicle events and customs. From such evidence we may be sure only that in those early days there were many motley tribes wandering this land of terrible storms and biting winds.

[164]

Commentary on Tartar Folk Tales

Every so often a tough and able leader brought many of these diverse tribes under his will, on occasion leading his armies to greener pastures along the great steppe highway, from what is now Mongolia through southern Russia into Central Europe. The conquering might of these nomads was felt from Russia to China, from India to Rome as, like ripples on a great lake, wave upon wave swept outwards to the west and to the east – Tartar, Mongol, Hun, Scythian and the rest.

The best known of these incursions began around AD 1220 when, from the far end of Asia, in the neighbourhood of Lake Baikal and the Gobi Desert, a fast-multiplying horde of Tartars descended to overrun the whole of Russia and much besides. They were led by one of the greatest leaders the world has ever known – Chingis Khan.

Perhaps we can see Chingis Khan's life in better perspective if we know what was happening in England during those same years. When Chingis was only twelve years old, Thomas à Becket was returning to England from exile. In 1189, when Chingis Khan was twenty-two, Richard the Lionheart came to the throne; and Richard's brother, King John, signed the Magna Carta nine years after Chingis Khan had first held his own parliament, the Grand Kuriltai. When Chingis died, at the age of sixty in 1227, King Henry III came of age.

In the year 1167 was born a son to Yesukai Bagadur, chief of a small clan of wandering shepherds known as Yakka Mongols. The son received the name Temuchin. But he was to become known to history as Chingis Khan, meaning 'Master of the World'. When Temuchin was a young man, his tribe, like many others, was subject to a Chinese governor, Ong-Khan. Temuchin was only thirteen when his father died, poisoned by a rival, and Temuchin himself had to lead the clan. At first deserted by his clansmen and hunted by enemies while struggling to keep his people together, he gradually built up both fame and power until he had welded together the entire nomadic peoples of Central Asia. Over a period of some twenty-five years Chingis Khan created a vast empire, sending out on all sides an avalanche of warriors, or 'raging torrents' as they were known by those they defeated, aiming at the dominion of the world. It was this multi-coloured tribal array of horse archers fighting under the standard of the Nine Yak-Tails that was given, in the thirteenth century, the name 'Tartar' by their principal foes, the Russians and the Chinese. The Russian

[165]

tatarin and the Chinese *ta-ta* were words that struck terror in the hearts of Russian and Chinese alike – and with good cause.

By the time he died, Chingis's empire stretched a quarter of the way round the world, from Peking to the Black Sea. Not long after, in 1258, his successors embraced Islam as their faith and the Tartar (Turkic) language as their common tongue – as cultural 'cement' to bind together the many tribes and clans that made up the Golden Horde. Chingis's descendants extended the empire even further.

In that area of the world that concerns us – the great Russian plain and Central Asia – Chingis's son and successor, Ogodai, granted to a nephew, Batu, the entire Russian territory from the Urals to the Dnieper River. With an enormous host of 300,000 men, Batu annihilated the kingdom of the Bolgars on the River Volga in 1236 and thrust forward all the way to Hungary, Poland and the Adriatic Sea.

Many are the tales and legends told of these brave and fierce Tartars. To be sure, it is often hard to unravel fact from fiction. Two Italian friars, Plano Carpini and Rubruquis, who journeyed eastwards six years after Russia's submission, described the ruined cities of Russia as being full of skulls and skeletons. Yet, on visiting the Tartars, the friars wrote that they were struck by the complete docility of the men and women; they never seemed to quarrel among themselves. All the same, after forty years of victorious war, like most conquerors, they seemed to despise other peoples and believed themselves destined to fulfil their leader's command to rule the world – not unlike the Romans in an earlier period or the British in a later one. It is said they showed no pity in battle, quoting a saying of Chingis Khan that 'regret is the fruit of pity'. In the old Russian city of Vladimir, the entire princely family, priests and townsfolk were burned to death in the cathedral in which they had taken refuge. To be fair to the Tartars it must be said that this was done at the instigation of a rival Russian prince, brother to the Prince of Vladimir. Yet, after a major battle, when the Tartars won the Russian capital, Kiev, all the Russian princes of that area and their families were rounded up; the Tartars were then said to have built a huge banqueting table on top of their captives and feasted above them, crushing them to death.

Notwithstanding their legendary savagery – often embroidered upon by their foes – the Tartars were a hardy, courageous and cultivated people. The Venetian traveller, Marco Polo, who lived in Tartary for seventeen years (1275–92) in the service of the famous Tartar emperor Kubla Khan, wrote that the Tartars could live for a month on nothing but mare's milk (kumis) from which they made a kind of porridge; if without other food, they would draw blood from their own veins. They could stay on horseback for two days at a time, and sleep while their horses grazed. During their campaigns each man took about eighteen horses with him, riding them in turn.

For over 200 years the Tartar Golden Horde dominated Russia until the 'Tartar yoke' was thrown off by the armies of the Russian tsar, Ivan the Terrible, which sacked the Tartar stronghold of Kazan in 1480. Soon afterwards the Golden Horde broke up, scattering pockets of Tartars about the Russian land, but mainly forming separate Tartar states or khanates in Central Asia.

Today Kazan is the capital of Tartarstan, the autonomous Tartar republic within the USSR in which half of the five million Tartars live. The other two major Tartar groups are to be found in southern Siberia and the Crimea. All these Tartars speak a common language with and are related to the peoples of the five Soviet republics of Central Asia: Uzbekistan, Kirgizia, Kazakhstan, Turkmenia and Tadzhikistan, which now occupy the land of Tartary from which our stories come.

> *What shall we tell you? Tales, marvellous tales*
> *Of ships and stars and isles where good men rest,*
> *Where nevermore the rose of sunset pales,*
> *And winds and shadows fall toward the West.*
> James Elroy Flecker, 'The Golden Journey to Samarkand'

TALES THE TARTARS TOLD

Tartar folklore is washed by a mighty ocean of Oriental influences, rich in sensuous fantasies and legends that were already old when Europe lay in cultural darkness. The Tartar, like the Arab, has at his command a full and poetical language which affords him a host of synonyms and similes to gloss over the roguish wit of the Russian peasant or the homely jest of the Anglo-Saxon villein. This is best expressed in the enormous number of songs, tales and sayings in which popular wit enlivens events and people with humour, smites with satire or boldly holds up to laughter.

It is this sparkling liveliness, inventiveness and downright cunning which

[167]

can gain a simple soul a meal or even a bride, as in stories featuring the wily Aldar-Kose: whenever a crafty folk hero is called for, it is invariably the ubiquitous Aldar-Kose who fits the bill. He wanders through folklore as far afield as Mongol and Kazakh, Kirgiz and Altai. In our collection he also turns up as the village joker in 'The Leaning Birch'. But wit and wiles, especially when employed in spinning tales, can also save lives, as with the woodman This-timelastyear in 'Shuralee' and with Yerensay. There are echoes in the latter of the storytelling of Shahrazad in *The Arabian Nights*, that vizier's lovely daughter who, to save her life, told the sultan a thousand tales so artfully that one adventure became tangled with another and the sultan could not be sure of knowing what happened in one tale unless he first listened to several other shorter stories.

More obviously akin to the harsh truths of a certain stage in Tartar history is the much-travelled theme in Tartar folklore of the killing of the sick and aged ('The Golden Vase'). This is likely to have originated in the custom among some nomadic tribes of putting weaklings – babies, the old and the infirm – to death because they were a burden on the tribe when moving or fighting. And, since food was scarce and swiftness vital, the food was kept for the strong and the fast-moving. The aged and the weak came to be despised.

Elements of the story 'Upon Jewel Mountain' have their echo in the real-life adventures of Hulagu, a grandson of Chingis Khan, who set out in 1253 to conquer northern Iran and Mesopotamia. By 1257 he had captured Alamut, the Eagle's Nest, in the Elbrus Mountains. The next year he took the holy city of Baghdad, the seat of the caliph (today capital of Iraq). The caliph himself was rolled in a carpet and, in order to avoid shedding royal blood – for that would have been a sin – he was trampled to death by several strong men.

One of Hulagu's foes in his conquest of the Eagle's Nest and the surrounding territories was Aladdin, the sheik or Old Man of the Mountains, supported by his attendant assassins. The traveller Marco Polo tells us how Aladdin held his court with great splendour and magnificence and bore himself most nobly, convincing the simple mountain folk that he was a prophet.

But the truth, Marco Polo explains, was rather different. In a valley between two mountains, Sheik Aladdin had made the biggest and most beautiful garden that was ever seen, planted with all the finest fruits and flowers in the world and containing the most splendid mansions and palaces, ornamented with gold and with likenesses of all that is beautiful on earth, and also four pipes, one flowing with wine, one with milk, one with honey and one with water. There were fair damsels, the loveliest in the world, unrivalled at playing every sort of instrument and at singing and dancing. Aladdin gave his men to understand that this garden was Paradise. At the entrance stood a fortress so strong that its inhabitants feared no army; and there was no other way in except through this fortress.

Into this garden the sheik would introduce carefully picked young men from the country around, having first rendered them insensible with hashish, the drug which gave them their name, *hashashin*, or assassins, in other words hashish-takers. When the young men awoke in the garden, they were convinced they had died and were in Paradise, particularly as the lovely maidens stayed with them all the while, singing and making music for their delight and ministering to their every desire. So these young men had all they could wish for and asked nothing better than to remain there.

But the Old Man of the Mountains had other plans for them. When he wanted emissaries to send on some mission of murder, he would administer the drug to as many as he pleased, and, while they slept, he had them carried into his palace and locked in a dark dungeon. When they came to they were sure they had indeed been in Paradise, and their only wish was to return there. The Old Man would tell them he had the means of sending them back, and would dispatch them on some dangerous mission of murder or assassination. The young men were filled with such a great desire to return to this Paradise that they longed for death, which would enable them to go there.

In this ingenious manner the Old Man built up a band of dedicated killers who cared not whether they died and whose ruthlessness made them the scourge of the entire area. Thus it happened, says Marco Polo, that no one ever escaped when the sheik wanted his death, and many kings and lords paid tribute to him and cultivated his friendship for fear that he might bring about their end.

But Chingis Khan's grandson, Hulagu, knowing of all the evil deeds of this sheik and making up his mind that he should be crushed, besieged him in his fortress of Alamut for three years and in the end captured and killed him. After their defeat by Hulagu, the Ismailis, as the Old Man's sect now called themselves, went into hiding and continued to carry out well-planned assassinations to obtain land and riches from frightened rulers. With the passage of time the

[169]

activities of the Ismailis became more respectable and today they take their lead from the Aga Khan, head of the Ismaili sect and direct descendant of the Old Man of the Mountains, Aladdin.

Features of this story are clearly to be found in 'Proud Ilbatyr in the Land of Cathay'. The great wall alluded to in 'Ilbatyr' is the Great Wall of China, Cathay being the name used by Marco Polo for China, and the wall having been built originally to keep out the marauding Tartars. It was Hulagu's brother, the famous Kubla Khan (1259–94) who became the first Tartar or 'barbarian' to rule over the whole of China.

Elements of 'The Tale of the Kurai', as of several Tartar tales, are symbolic. One such is the roll made with human milk: the person who eats it becomes the son of the hero's mother or wife, or his 'milk-brother'. The horn in this story has a sinister ring (as also in 'The Tale of the Three Talismans'), though generally in Oriental myth, the horn is a symbol of superhuman power, virility and good fortune. When the bearer loses his horn or tusk, he, like Sampson shorn of his hair, forfeits his great power and strength. In the story of the kurai, however, these elements seem to be merely trappings embellishing the main theme: to explain the origin of the flute-like instrument popular among several Tartar peoples, particularly the Bashkirs.

Water has a magical significance in a number of tales, as it generally does in folklore: in 'Abzelil and the Master of the Lake' the waters of the lake are guarded by an evil giant, master of the horses of the lake; in 'Altyn Saka', of which many versions exist, the great lake is watched over by the hideous witch, Ubyr, whose steed is summoned from the lake; in 'Shaitan the Devil and his Forty Daughters' a white swan is seized by a black witch on a lake. To the superstitious Tartar mind, water represented the nether world inhabited by the souls of the departed. The evil force guarding the watery depths is the watchman over the kingdom of the dead, keeping their peace and punishing any intruder. The dead awakened from their slumbers take on the forms of horses. In some Tartar tales the pagan Shaitan has become Iblis, who, according to the Koran, had been an angel whom Allah had created from fire but then expelled from Paradise for his misdemeanours.

As with all folk tales, many Tartar stories have their origin in actual history, recounted and embroidered down the ages by the Tartar *sesens* or jesters, by grandmothers and other such founts of oral wisdom. These tales are not, we must remember, archaeological remains – they are living things, not fossils. They expand and shrink on their journey down the years. All the same, they tell us something of the history of the people; they reflect their feats and suspicions, their ideals of beauty and honour. The Tartar tales have been shaped and indelibly etched by the climate, the terrain, the feuds with other tribes, the social order, the mixture of ancient myth, Mohammedan faith and mystical images from other religions that crossed their path.

My own introduction to Tartar folklore has a ring of fantasy about it. One chill February evening some years ago, when I was working in Moscow, a knock came at the door of my apartment. The door opened to reveal a young girl, dark-haired, almond-eyed, a proud daughter of Tartary. She had journeyed from Bashkiria, it turned out, to visit her Kirgiz cousin who had occupied the apartment before me. Finally she located her relative and subsequently acted as my guide and interpreter on tours of Central Asia, Bashkiria and Tartarstan. It was from some of her hospitable elders in Tartar auls beside the River Byeli that, over the traditional fish-head and frothy mares' milk given to honoured guests, I jotted down versions of a number of these tales ('Aldar-Kose', 'Shura-lee', 'Abzelil', 'Kurai'); now and then I also had the good fortune to disturb the dusty slumbers of books of legends on shelves of Tartar cottages. It is from these main sources, and from the lips of my Tartar wife (for so my guide became) and mother-in-law, that the stories in this first English collection of Tartar folk tales are taken.

It is, then, with much fondness and gratitude that I dedicate this labour of love to Rashida and our children Salavat, Onara and Gulnara, joint descendants of Chingis Khan and Saint Patrick, and to all those who would dare take the Golden Road to Samarkand.

JAMES RIORDAN

Verkhneye Yarkeyevo – Bradford
1977

Books Consulted

Tatarskie narodnye skazki (Tartar Folk Tales), K. Yarmukhametov (ed.), Kazan, 1970

Bashkirskie narodnye skazki (Bashkir Folk Tales), A. Usmanov (ed.), Ufa, 1969

Kazakhsky folklor v sobranii G. N. Potanina (Kazakh Folklore Collected by G. N. Potanin), Alma Ata, 1972

Iz istorii Tatarii (From the History of Tartary), N. Munkov, Kazan, 1970

Chudesny sad. Kazakhskie narodnye skazki (The Wonderful Garden. Kazakh Folk Tales), Y. Malyuga (ed.), Leningrad, 1970

Khozyain vetrov. Skazki narodov RSFSR (Lord of the Winds. Folk Tales of the Peoples of the Russian Republic), M. Bulatov (ed.), Moscow, 1965

Skazki (Tales), B. Karamzin (ed.), Ufa, 1974

A Thousand Years of the Tartars, E. H. Parker, London, 1924

Recollections of Tartar Steppes, L. Atkinson, London, 1863

Essays on Tatar History, B. Ischboldin, New Delhi, 1963

Histoire des Tartares, Simon de Saint-Quentin, Paris, 1965

A Journey in Southern Siberia, Jeremiah Curtin, Boston, 1909

The Story of Genghis Khan, Charles King, London, 1971

To the Back of Beyond, Fitzroy Maclean, London, 1974

Pedestrian Journey through Russia and Siberian Tartary, J. D. Cochrane, London, 1825